THE PEARL DROP KILLER

JOSHUA QUENTIN HAWK

Other books by Joshua Quentin Hawk

The Lost Outpost

Contents

A Killing Field 1

Back on the Job 16

Interviews... 29

The Pearl Drop Club... 44

The Investigation... 58

Suspects 71

Playthings... 88

Survivors 110

History... 124

Last Pieces.. 140

Endgame 155

A Killing Field

In a damp meadow on a cool spring morning, as the Sun rose in the sleepy fishing town of Jackson Hole, small patches of snow were still on the ground as the Sun continued through the forest onto the bay. The wind rustled through the shrubs and treetops. A small white mutt of a dog, no one owns but everyone cares for, and feeds, scurried out of the shrubs with a woman's left hand, in his mouth. He ran up to a man, around sixty, with gray shaggy hair and a long shaggy beard, wearing a bright yellow raincoat, pants, and cap, and heading down toward the piers along the bay to start his day, smoking his corncob pipe, carrying four fishing rods. The dog dropped the hand and barked a few times, getting the old man's attention. He turned back toward the dog, stooped down, petted him, and saw the hand.

"What you got there, boy?" The old man asked as he picked the hand up slowly, barely holding on to it by his index finger and thumb. "And where did you find this?" The dog barked a few more times and ran back to the shrubs that he came out of, sat, and barked some more for the old man to follow him. He pushed the shrubs away, "What you got in there, boy?" As he looked down into the shrubs, he stumbled with fright and fell.

A young girl, sixteen, blond, and white, wearing a string of teardrop pearls around her neck, and dressed in a white ball gown, with heavy makeup on, as if she just came from a debutant ball. Her lifeless green eyes just stared up at him, and her left hand was cut off, which the dog found, and with surgical precision, the man turned to his side, vomited, and dropped the hand.

Jackson Hole Deputies, dressed in khaki slacks, khaki short-sleeve dress shirts, with brown pocket flaps, taped off the area and started searching the woods. A black Jeep Grand Cherokee, SUV sped up with its red lights flashing in the back window. A tall late forties heavyset man dressed in a nice black suit, and as if he had slept in it, with no tie and thinning black hair combed straight back—a really bad dye job— stepped out. His partner, an African American woman, in her late twenties, with long black hair down past her shoulders and a set of even bangs along her forehead, wearing a black business suit, quickly walked up to the tapeline where two deputies were standing and talking with an older deputy, with sergeant stripes. He raised his gold shield, a seven-point gold shield with blue lettering, "JACKSON HOLE COUNTY," and with the rank of Lieutenant. "Lieutenant O'Malley, and Sergeant Stein," he advised the young man and then pointed back toward his partner as the young man raised the tape.

They stepped up to the older officer, in his fifties, Sergeant with three stripes on his sleeves, white with dark olive skin, and bald. "How the hell did they drag out of bed this early, O'Malley? You're normally closing the bars."

"Nice one, Duke. My new partner, Dana Stein. What you got?" O'Malley asked as he stooped down over the body, the shrubs had been cleared away.

"I think it's called a Crime Scene, Lieutenant," Duke replied, and Stein smiled.

"Where is the Crime Scene Unit?" O'Malley said, looking right at him and found finding none of this funny.

He took a pair of gloves from his coat pocket and picked up the young girl's hand.

"Not here yet, a record for you, the first time you have beaten them," Duke commented.

O'Malley stood and was about to crack one of his jokes, when another male deputy's voice called out, "Got another one!" O'Malley and Stein started walking and moved past Duke, and continued toward the deputy's voice, and a different female deputy called out over O'Malley's left shoulder with another body. O'Malley pointed for Stein to continue on the new call, and four more Deputies called out, O'Malley looked back at Duke, each man knew this was not good, "Get all hands on deck, Duke."

O'Malley waved Stein to continue, and he continued to the second one, a female deputy, with red hair, Corporal stripes, and two chevrons on her sleeves, pointed to an area between her and him, he stooped down. A sixteen-year-old girl, white, this time in a black dress, a string of teardrop pearls around her neck, and left hand cut off, and missing this time, heavy makeup as the first. He moved the foliage around, looking, but no sign of her hand, "Mark it," he ordered pointing to the body and then back to the Corporal, and headed back toward Stein.

Stein was stooping over another young woman in her early twenties, white dress, teardrop pearl necklace, and her left hand surgically removed and missing, and like the others, with heavy makeup.

"Mark it," Stein informed the young African American deputy standing near her and moved off to the next body, another young woman in her twenties, black dress, teardrop pearl necklace, left hand cut off and missing. O'Malley stooped, noticing this woman had been here for some time, there was more decomposition, animal bites, and her eyes had been eaten out, and parts of her thighs, and arms gnawed at. A week or more, he thought.

They continued to the next one, same description: in her twenties, left hand surgically removed and missing, with a teardrop pearl necklace and ball gown, more recent like the first one. He looked over at Stein and then up at the deputy. He looked around more and then back at the deputy near him, rubbed his face slowly, thinking. Seven girls, he had seen this before, and hoped he would never have seen it again, and knew they would need Donovan's help.

"What is this?" Stein asked.

He stood and looked back down at the girl and then back up at Stein. "A killing field, a dumping ground. We have ourselves a serial killer?"

Duke joined them coming through some high scrubs behind them. "The Captain is on her way, and as many as she could, to help. How many we got?"

O'Malley looked at the deputy. "I heard about six calls out, Sir."

"Seven. I want a ten-by-ten-mile radius perimeter, Duke, and no damn press!" He walked past Duke, heading back to his SUV with Stein following.

"Have you worked a serial before?" Stein asked.

"Yeah, but not like this bad. But I know someone who has." As he reached for the tape, raised it, and walked up to his SUV, he pulled a map out of the glove box, under a whiskey bottle, which looked half empty, opened the map over the hood of the Jeep.

Captain Sarah MacBride pushed her way through the crowd of Deputies, her red hair emerging from the sea of brown hats like a beacon. Though she looks tough in her black business suit, the pink blouse she wears beneath offers a hint of her softer side. In her forties, MacBride has seen it all, and the stress showed in the wrinkles around her eyes as she yanked her sunglasses off. "What we got, O'Malley? Duke said all hands on deck."

"We have found seven bodies, anywhere from last night to maybe about a month ago—a dumping ground," he answered just as three more deputies called out, "Make that ten."

"Serial killer?"

"Looks that way. We'll know more after CSU processes the scenes," he said as he circled another area on the map. "You know, if Donovan was still on the force, he could be a big help."

She knew that was true, but she did not wish to believe it. Stein watched them and stepped up to Duke, who had now returned to the base camp. "Who are they talking about?"

"Donovan, O'Malley's ex-partner." Duke answered.

"I heard he retired?"

"She fired him. The best damn Forensic Psychologist and investigator we ever had—ex-FBI. She didn't like how he was handling a murder case two years ago. She said, she thought he was taking his sweet time. It was politics and she fired him, it took O'Malley and six other detectives, from three nearby counties, to find that bastard, and took almost another year, right where Donovan said he would be, and what he was doing with the last victim. If she had let him do his job in the first place, then we could have saved the other six girls of the eight he killed," Duke explained in a fatherly way.

MacBride heard Duke, knowing he was right, "You'll call him, right?" MacBride asked trying to get on O'Malley's good side.

Without looking up from the map, "You married him, you divorced him, and you fired him. That's all on you, Sarah," as he picked up the map and walked back over to Duke and Stein, showed him the map of the areas to search. Duke took the map, and with several other deputies, they all headed off into the forest.

"Any word on CSU?" O'Malley asked.

"Right there." Stein said pointing over his shoulder, as two black vans and a white one pulled up, four women and two men climbed out of the vans in light blue jumpsuits, labeled, "CSU" on their backs. One of the women had brunette hair, just past her shoulders and she walked up to O'Malley, with the Medical Examiner on her back, who now returned the first victim, and looked her over again.

"I heard it's a big one?" She said.

"Duke will assign areas, we have ten bodies so far," O'Malley said as he waved all but the brunette toward Duke. "This is victim one. From what I can tell, is the first one was dropped within the last twenty-four hours. We'll know more from your reports. Some have been here for weeks, a few others maybe a month, I think."

She stooped down and looked over the body. MacBride walks up, "You got this?" as she puts her cell phone back in her pocket.

"Yeah," O'Malley replied without looking up as he pulled his cell phone out. "He is not answering, so I am going to have to find him," MacBride told O'Malley.

"Try the Roadhouse. I've seen him there a few times since the divorce; has a trailer there," O'Malley said without looking up at her, pondering over the scene.

She walked off and Stein stooped down with gloves, and picked up some small flakes of metal, yellow in color, near the severed wrist. She put them in an evidence bag from her pocket and passed it to the brunette, who looked up and saw the bag, took the bag from her, and their eyes locked.

They looked each other over, hoping no one saw them, both smiled.

O'Malley stepped away from the body, dialing his cell phone. "We have ten. She's coming to grovel … Yeah." He hung up his phone and put it back in his pocket.

The CSU team passed by him again with their kits, gloves, and a couple with masks covering their faces.

"O'Malley?" A tall African American man in his late forties, Richard McKnight, head of Forensics, bald with a black goatee, in a nice black three-piece suit, and vest, two large rings on his left hand, yelled out and waved from across the dirt road. He was also wearing black frame glasses. "I see my team is here. What you got?"

O'Malley raised the tape and walked toward him, and then saw the reporters down the road. As he stepped up to him, he said, "Serial Killer. We have found ten bodies so far, ranging from last night till about a month ago."

"Well, Alice Roberts, the county's best M.E. and best in her field, anything else my department can do, let me know," McKnight said, walking back to his nice vintage black Lincoln Continental. "And we could sure use Donovan on this!"

"She's on it," O'Malley said. McKnight looked at him and was in shock that she was going to ask Donovan, knowing that was a first. She was one who never asked whether it was done or required, a virtue she had acquired since she had been promoted to Captain and Chief of Detectives.

"O'Malley?" A young woman, blonde, in her mid-thirties, short gray skirt and a business jacket, stood next to a man with a TV camera, jeans, and a white T-shirt, among other reports behind a second tape line. "Any comments? We've heard a serial killer. Can you confirm?"

O'Malley whistled loud toward four deputies standing near the second tape line not doing their job with the reporters, motioned with his hands to push them back. "Ten, no, twenty feet!"

He turned back toward the forest and looked up. "I am too old for this crap, Roberta told me to give this shit up years ago."

Stein ran back toward him. "We got four more, a total of fourteen ranging from sixteen to twenty-five, according to Alice." O'Malley ran back the best he could with his bad knees, following her into the forest.

T.K. Donovan came sailing out the Roadhouse Grill's front large window, an old Roadhouse club and grill with large white stone walls, right out of the fifties, large neon sign on the roof. With a white double-sided set of doors on a freezer unit for bags of ice out front, and a large seven-foot-tall carved Indian near the front entrance, as they have outside old tobacco shops, next to the large, oversized window. A large dirt area out front for a parking lot with two old rotary-style gas pumps right out of the twenties or thirties, out near the blacktop, neither working anymore. Donovan in his forties but could pass for thirty, "And stay out!" the burly large man in his sixties, the cook, and wearing a white sailor's cap, white T-shirt, and blue jeans, called from inside. Donovan rolled over and sat up facing the bar. "But, I own it!"

"Then sober up!" the man yelled back, laughing.

MacBride's black Ford Crown Victoria sedan rolled up with red lights flashing in the back window and along the front grill, and she chirped her siren twice and stopped just shy of Donovan's head.

MacBride stepped out and waved over at the cook. "Hi, Daddy," She said as he moved back inside. Donovan turned his head back and up toward her, shielding his eyes from the bright Sun over his shoulder, and his massive headache from his hangover. "I have nothing to say to you," as he stood up, losing his balance, and leaned against the car, then wobbling off back toward the Roadhouse.

"I was wrong," she yelled.

He stopped, turned back, and put a hand up to his ear, "What?"

"I was wrong Donovan. I should have left you on the case."

"You only apologize when you need something, and *no* thank you," as he continued off to the side of the building. Up to his trailer, and long fifth-wheel mobile home, white with green and black waves, with a nineteen-fifties red Chevy pickup truck in front, a real classic, and urinates under the bunk section.

Rolling her eyes and yelled, "Donovan! O'Malley has ten bodies, in Sherman's Forest."

He paused, scratched his two-week growth of brown facial hair, and looked back over at her, but still leaning against the trailer and continued to urinate, "What's the catch? I come with you, and you put me on a bus of town. You always hated working with me."

"I hated living with you, not working with you. Please?"

"Please," he laughed. "Okay, okay," as he stumbled back to her car.

"Donovan!" she yelled then pointed down at his zipper that was still open, and then looked away with embarrassment.

He stopped, looked down at his oversized orange cargo shorts and black tee shirt, and then saw his zipper open. He turned around quickly, zipped it up, adjusting his crotch.

She rolled her eyes, then stumbled around toward the driver's door.

"Oh, hell no, no you don't Mister. Coffee first!" she yelled and turned him around and walked him back to the bar. "Daddy, black coffee, and strong!"

The cook, now back at the window, watching this farce between them, and just laughing, and then tossed a white towel onto his right shoulder. "Yes, baby."

"Why does your dad hate me so much?" he asked, breathing on her, she turned his face away.

At the counter and after many cups of coffee later, Donovan now resting his head on the bar, which was over eight feet on one side, and four on the other, with a black countertop and black padding along the edge. With a good-sized pass-through window and many bottles around it. "Daddy, why did you throw him out the window?"

Jock MacBride walked back down the bar toward them. "Do I need a reason with this *bum*?"

"This *bum* was the Father of your Granddaughters!"

"He tried to sell me a bill of goods, some land he has in
Colorado."

Before Jock could finish, she slapped Donavon on the back of his head. He jumped and sat up, "You Bastard! How many times have I told you not to screw with my Dad? He is a Golden Gloves champion for six years running. Next time, I will leave you on the ground. And that land was for Marci and Gina, *your* Daughters,"

"He knew I was kidding," Donovan replied, pointing at Jock.

"I did and I needed to fix that window anyway—cheaper if broken first," Jock giggled as he walked off through a set of double doors at the far end of the bar and back into the kitchen.

"Stop messing with my Dad, please?" "I own this bar; he works for me,"

"He just lost Mom, and you won it in a poker game because you had a better hand. Get over it."

"Okay, okay. What do you mean O'Malley has ten bodies in Sherman's Forest?" He asked well pouring another cup of coffee from a pitcher.

"He was called to a body dump early this morning, and so far, has found ten young women, ranging from last night to a month ago. We need your help."

Sipping from his cup, Donovan said, "Say, please?"

A shiver ran down her back, "I am not playing this game."

"Say, please?"

"Okay, please."

"Pretty please with sugar on top?" Donovan said with a smile on his face.

She rolled her eyes and shrugged her shoulders, "Fine! Pretty please with sugar on top. Fine, you happy?"

Jock returned from the kitchen, handed Donovan a fifty, and she looked at him, then Donovan, as Jock tossed him a pair of black jeans, put his black leather boots on the bar, and then lend over the bar toward her. "Get him out of here," he said, with his left thumb pointing at the front door by the large broken window.

Putting his pants on, she stood waiting near the front on the driver's side. "So what was that with Dad and the fifty bucks?"

"Before you came, he bet me I could get you to say, pretty please with sugar on top."

"How did you know I was coming?" she started, but she already knew the answer: O'Malley.

Laughing, "I knew you would have only done it if you thought I was messing with your Dad, so when we saw you driving up, I told him to toss me out the window. He was more than happy to oblige."

She looked back at the bar. Her Dad was still standing at the window, and waved at her with a big smile on his face. "You're both children!" she yelled and climbed in the driver's seat, and sped off. With Donovan's side door still open, and it shut quickly, she spun around onto the blacktop and raced down the road.

"So, what can you tell me about the scene?"

"I got a call from Duke, one of the first on the scene, and O'Malley had bodies, and to get all hands on deck. By the time I got there, he had found ten. CSU had not arrived and he, Stein, and half the department were still securing the scene. He called you?"

"Yeah, I knew that it would eat you up."

"I'll get him."

"Another time love," Donovan said putting his boots on.

"Don't call me that!"

"Okay, okay, let it go for now."

Her phone rang, and she pressed a button on the steering wheel. "Did you find him?" O'Malley asked.

"You two are both children! What am I going to do with you both?"

"What you got?" Donovan said speaking over her.

"Fourteen so far, I am going to need your help, T."

"On my way. What can you tell me?"

"Fourteen young women, sixteen to twenty-five, all dressed in fancy dresses, white or black, teardrop pearl necklaces, and get this, their left hands are cut off and missing, except the first one that a dog found."

Something in the back of Donovan's mind recognized the outfits and necklaces, but he could not place them. "Did you get the dog's statement?" Donovan asked, MacBride turned to him with her eyes wide open, swerving, catching herself, nearly hitting a tanker truck, and moving back onto her side of the road, as the tanker sounded.

"Yeah, bark, bark, bark bark." She pressed a button, turning the phone off, "Will you grow up and take this seriously?"

"If the dog took it, we would need to swab its mouth for trace."

She looked at him. He may be drunk and an ass at times, but sometimes he thinks of the oddest things that can help a case. "As a Consultant or Detective?" Donovan asked looking right at her

She opens the case between the seats and hands him his shield and gun, a navy SIG226 still in its holster. "I could never turn them in. Can you follow orders this time?"

"Can you leave the politics out of it?"

After a long pause, she bites her upper lip. "I will try."

"I will too, Captain MacBride."

For the first time, she felt that he truly meant it and heard the respect in his voice. "Where do you want to start?"

"I need to see the scene."

"Thought you would say that," MacBride said as she pulled up near the reporters. A deputy pulled one of the two barricades aside, and she drove through, pulling up near O'Malley's SUV and a few other patrol cars, white with a blue stripe running down their sides, and JACKSON HOLE COUNTY printed on the bumpers.

Donovan looked around, stepped out of the sedan, and handed him a stick of gum. They come around the car and step up to the tape, at the same time Duke is returning with three deputies.

"Good to have you back, nephew," Duke said, raising the tape for them to enter and giving MacBride a half-look, as if about time.

"Where's the first girl, Unc?" Donovan said, greeting his Uncle with a hug, and then he walked them back to the first girl, where the CSU was about to pick the body up and put her on a gurney, he put his hand out for them to wait. Stooped down for a better look and moved some leaves and twigs with a pen, that he took from MacBride's inside coat pocket. "All are the same?"

"Except for their ages and age of decomposition, and the color of their dresses, and this one with her hand, yes?" Alice explained.

"What colors?"

"White like hers or black," Alice replied.

"I have seen this outfit and pearls before," Donovan commented under his breath, but before anyone could answer, O'Malley and Stein returned to the scene.

"About damn time, T," O'Malley said looking at the group, then at MacBride.

Donovan looked up as they returned. "Still only fourteen, O'Malley?"

"Yeah, I have them looking an additional five miles in all directions."

Alice and another tech pick the body up and transfer it to a body bag, and then onto a gurney. "Wait," O'Malley said watching a small white card falling to the ground. He quickly picks it up, turns it over, and shows it to Stein, she looks at MacBride, and O'Malley gives it to Donovan.

Donovan puts his hand out toward Alice. "Glove, please?" Alice hands him one from her pocket. He slips it on and takes the card, flips it over, nothing on the back. "It's one of my Dad's. Bag it, run it, and make sure you are careful with the others; may also have something hidden."

Alice nodded and placed it in an evidence bag, she took it out from her oversized black kit, filled it out on the front, and closed the body bag around the young girl. Donovan looks over the ground. "Okay, where is the oldest one?"

"Over this way, by the creek," O'Malley said, heading off.

Donovan and MacBride follow Stein and O'Malley back deep into the woods to a point near a creek. MacBride vomited seeing the body's decomposition: the woman's face mostly gnawed off, her eyes and nose missing, and a lot of dried blood. A few maggots have worked their way around under what skin remains of her face. Donovan shoves her a bit to the right but held onto her, so she does not vomit near the body and contaminate the scene.

"We have called for Forensic Anthropologists from the University to help," Stein said.

"Good, leave the ones that are at least three weeks old or older, so they can judge the full decomp," Donovan ordered, stooping down for a better look.

"Any witnesses?" Donavan asked.

"A fisherman, whom the dog found with the hand, a ranger that was through this area about three hours earlier," O'Malley reported.

"We still have the dog?" Donovan asked looking up at him.

Stein looked puzzled. "Why?"

"There may be some trance in the dog's mouth from the hand," MacBride explained as if a student who knows the answer, blurts it out, as she wipes her mouth with a white handkerchief, O'Malley handed her. Donovan smiled and continued to look around.

"Where's the ranger?" Donovan asked.

"After we took his statement, he needed to finish his rounds up in the forest," O'Malley answered.

"I'll want to talk to him," Donovan said, stooping over the woman and looking around.

O'Malley nodded, Donovan walked back into the woods, back toward base camp with MacBride following him. "Anyone for Sushi?"

"Keep it up!" MacBride yelled, slapping Donovan on his back, and now Stein vomited. O'Malley grabbed her by the waist and moved her from the area.

"Document, Document, Document!" Donovan yelled back.

O'Malley just holds Stein by her arm and waist, as she continues to vomit, "Good to have you back, T."

Back on the Job

Donovan and MacBride entered the station, walked down a small corridor, and up to the check-in desk, four and a half feet tall, with a small swinging door on one side and a long wooden bench to their right. A young girl, looking right out of high school, Maria Ramirez, just shy of five foot nothing, black hair, sat at the check-in desk, with four other deputies around her, she ran around the desk, hugging Donovan. The others see him and start clapping, to celebrate his return, "Okay, okay, back to work. It's not like he is the prodigal son or something," MacBride said.

"Your back?" Maria asked, stepping back some.

"For this case, so far, I think," Donovan said, looking over at MacBride.

MacBride pointed to keep him moving, and they continued into the bullpen. A few of the deputies welcomed him back with pats on his shoulder and handshakes, and he noticed O'Malley's desk. The messy one in the place, except for a small area in the top right-hand corner, a single picture frame. A photo of a young Hispanic woman in her forties, with dark hair—Roberta, O'Malley's wife—and two-wallet size pictures: one of a boy about eight, in a blue and white Little League uniform, with brown hair, kneeling with a bat. A young girl, about seven in a white ballet leotard, with blonde hair and looking across the way, seeing his old desk, which was now Stein's. It was immaculate, still not lived in, since she just started a couple of days ago. He looked around for an empty desk.

"This way, Mister," MacBride said, walking him over to an empty office next to hers along the back wall.

"I'm moving up in the world," Donovan said, entering the room.

"As you said, we'll see," MacBride said, watching him sit down behind the desk. "This could work," Donovan said, sitting back in the chair, finally in his father's office.

Maria entered with a cup of coffee. "Here you go, black just like you like it." She turned and saw the look on MacBride's face, who nodded toward the door, and Maria left quickly.

"Where do you want to start?" MacBride asked.

"Hanson!" Donovan yelled, moving around the desk toward the door.

Charles Hanson, mid-thirties, corporal stripes on his sleeves, one of the young deputies with Duke at the crime scene, when O'Malley arrived, entered his office. "I need everything on the Sherman's Forest—any recent deaths and missing person's reports of young women and teen girls, say . . . the last six months," Donovan asked. Hanson nodded and left.

"Well, just move right in," MacBride said, both giggling, and she returned to her own office.

Donovan grabbed his old whiteboard from the bullpen in the corner near his office, by a long table sitting up against the wall, which had a list of deputies' names and shift times—their roll sheet. Erased it and pulled it into his office, wrote on it: 14 female bodies, 16-25 years old, black/white dresses, pearl drop necklaces, along the top of the board. "I have seen these outfits with pearls before," commenting to himself as he writes 'Left hands cut off like surgeon on the lower right side of the board.

"Already down to business, I like that," O'Malley said, standing in the doorway, Donovan paused looking over the board, then turned back toward him. O'Malley handed him a few brown folders, "First reports from the scenes. Stein will have the rest and photographs soon." as he then handed a few of the files he had.

"Good, have you been able to let the ranger know I wish to talk to him?" Donovan asked taking the folders.

"I am to meet him at the ranger station at two p.m. I will have him here at eight a.m. when he gets off shift."

"Good," Donovan answered skimming the first folder.

"I meant what I said, T. It's good to have you back."

"I hope Dana is working out?" Donovan said still not looking up at him and leaning against his desk, reading one of the files.

"She'll be fine. She's a good detective."

"Good detective?" Donovan said, looking up with some shock. "You said, a woman could never be a *good* detective well enough for you, while you were on the job."

"Yeah I know, but she has been a good help on many of my cases, well she was still in the academy. Guess you mellowed me."

Donovan dropped the files on the desk behind him, and O'Malley sat down on the long old green worn-out, fabric couch. "How long do the Forensic Anthropologists say they needed for analysis?"

"A few days, same as Alice," O'Malley answered as he put his feet up on the small wooden coffee table.

"Get me the photographs as soon as you can," Donovan said, sitting back behind his desk.

O'Malley stood quickly, thinking he could have sat for a time, then walked out, remembering Donovan was always focused, when on the job. Hanson returned with two file boxes. "Here you go, sir. The missing persons, teens, and twenties, over the last six months, and Jane Does, deceased last six months. Not a lot here," he said as he placed the papers on top of Sherman's forest with maps, "only been a park for about twenty years; before that, it was owned by the Sherman family."

"Any of them left?" Donovan asked still skimming O'Malley's folders.

"Old Lady Sherman is still alive, eighty years old, up in the old house, north of the park with her Daughter, fifty-something, and a few nurses. There is a Granddaughter, but no one has seen her for a couple of years." Hanson said, skimming the first pages.

"Any more information you get on the family and the Granddaughter, let me know," Donovan asked, looking up at him.

"Yes, Sir," Hanson said and left.

MacBride returned, seeing the board and boxes. "One thing I did like about working with you, you never left a stone unturned," she said, but not sure, if he was listening, and left. Stein entered wheeling a dolly with five boxes. "Here are the last reports other than M.E.'s and the Anthropologists, and photos are in the front of each folder, as you like, instructed by Duke. Forensics should be back in a day or two, according to Richard."

"You have copies?" Donovan asked looking up, as she entered. "Yes, copies have been made."

"Good, missing persons and death notices of teens and twenty-something women," Donovan said placing his hand on one of the boxes Hanson gave him. "Start comparing photos from the crime scenes, pull any deputies you need," Donovan said, while still reading over reports O'Malley gave him.

She added the two boxes to the others on her dolly and wheeled them out and into the conference room. She poked her head out and saw two female deputies and three male deputies, standing by the coffee maker, near the long table across the room. "You five, in here. Scott, coffee, two sugars."

They moved to the conference room, Scott, the red-haired deputy first seen at the crime scene, makes her coffee and then joins them. Donovan stepped out of his office and saw her instructing the deputies on matching photos and reports to missing and deceased victims, and joined MacBride in her office. "Stein seems quite capable?"

"Top of her class at the academy. FBI asked for her, but she wanted a small town to start in," MacBride answered, still signing reports.

"Kind of how you started?" Donovan said.

"Yes, did you need something?" still without looking up at him.

"I have been thinking. I'd like to buy you dinner, so we can start over."

"No strings attached?"

"Not from me, but you know your Dad."

"Will I need a witness?" MacBride asked, finally looking up at him.

The Sun was setting through the repaired window of the Roadhouse Grill. MacBride found one table in the middle, set with a white tablecloth; the pool tables in the back down a few steps are covered in the back. The lights for the booth sections were also off, and two long-stemmed white candles flicked in the dimmed light. Donovan came from behind the bar, and was now clean-shaven, in a nice black suit and white dress shirt, no tie. MacBride had changed also, wearing a blue spaghetti-strapped dress, down past her knees, and two-inch heels. "We are busy tonight, but I think I could squeeze you in, Madam," Donovan said, taking her hand and leading her to the table. He still loves her.

"Sit already, you bum. Dinner's getting cold," Jock called out from the kitchen they can tell he does not wish to be there.

She laughs, and he pulls her chair out, helps her with her chair, and sits, "So what's the catch, Donovan?"

"You came and apologized, and I was an ass. So, I thought I would try to make it up to you," he said.

Jock dropped two plates of spaghetti on the table. "Will you two just kiss and make up already, and stop this shadow dancing," he grunted and returned to the kitchen.

"Stay in the kitchen old man or leave!"

"Donovan!"

"Ok, I am sorry."

"What have you come up with so far?" she asked, changing the subject.

"Dana has done a good job, and her teams have already found five of the missing girls and have matched them to five of our victims."
"That's good, what's your next step?" she asked, eating the spaghetti, to keep him talking so he does not upset her father anymore. Pouring some red wine, "I instructed her to take a few deputies and talk to the families, and learn what they can about the missing girls, and

if anything of the last days of each girl, and what each was up to at the time they were reported missing, or anything out of the ordinary." He explained, sipping his wine.

"That's good."

"O'Malley has set up a time tomorrow for me and him to meet with the Ranger, at the station, around eight a.m."

Jock started cleaning glasses behind the bar, "Should I lock up?"

Both giggled, Donovan turned fast, to face him. "You may go, Jock, I'll lock up, and thank you." Jock shrugged his shoulder, grunted, and grabbed his cap from his back pocket, and left through the front door.

MacBride smiled as he turned back. "What what did I do now?" he asked.

"Nothing, I do feel better you're on the case. Hope you can forgive me for the termination?"

"I don't blame you. I blame the city council but do understand their reasons and the families wanting answers, which I did not have. But investigations take time."

"Any help you need from me?" she asked, sipping some more wine.

"Just keep the press and council off my ass till I know a bit more after all the autopsies and family interviews. For now, it's an open investigation, once we know something, we'll let them know. Is the party line, no special interviews with the press or council, and inform the department for me?"

"I can do that."

His phone rang and he pulled it from his right coat pocket. "Hello, ok, on our way," putting his phone back in his coat pocket. "Duke just found three more bodies. O'Malley and Stein are on their way."

"Where?"

"Sherman Cemetery." They quickly clean up and run out. Jock came out of the kitchen. "I have been cleaning up after her since she was in diapers. Nothing new."

MacBride slowly drove her black sedan up the path through the cemetery gates, past two deputies, to a second area taped off with vehicles and flashing lights, deputies searching the grounds. O'Malley was leaning against his SUV looking over his small notebook, there were two black vans across from him, as he put his notebooks in his left coat pocket, quickly pulled out a flask, took a quick drink, and put its back into his inside coat pocket, hoping no one had seen him.

"Duke said three more?" Donovan said as he put his jacket on, and she slipped on flats.

"Sorry to interrupt your date. This way. Alice has not moved anything and is waiting." They followed O'Malley up the hillside over many flat headstones, to where Stein and Roberts were waiting near a large headstone:

SHERMAN

Horace 'The Ol Jackal' Jackson Beauregard

1925 – 1995

Two twenty-something women, and an eighteen-year-old, are lying in a row, the twenty-something women are in black dresses on either side of the sixteen-year-old, in white, eighteen-year-old has both her hands. All three with pearls drop necklaces, Alice was waiting on her knees near one of the women in black, across from them as they came up. Stein and Scott near the headstone, Scott is holding an oversized camera with a large flashbulb unit, connected to a long metal bar on its base.

Alice points at the girl near her and then the one past the younger girl. "These two have been dead about ten hours, rigor is subsiding, the other one, has been dead less than five hours, rigor is still active," Alice reported pointing at the one in the middle.

Donovan stepped over near Alice, looked over the bodies, and pulled out gloves from his jacket pocket.

"We were about to move the bodies and see if anything falls out like the first one," Stein said waving at two techs, who were already bringing in two gurneys and body bags.

"Start with these two," Donovan waved at the two in black dresses, "Since they are older."

Alice and the male tech slowly took the first girl by the shoulders and legs and placed her up on the gurney and into a body bag, nothing dropped out, he wheeled the gurney away, and another tech helped Alice with the other girl and still nothing fell and wheeled the gurney away.

"You've gotten photos of the girls before I got here?" Donovan asked looking at Scott.

"Yes, and now, I will get to the ground where they were lying," Scott answered moving around Stein near the remaining body and waiting.

"Get a few of the headstones, please?" Donovan asked, stepping out of the way for the techs to bring in another gurney.

Scott nodded and the first tech returned for the last body, Alice and the tech picked up the last girl, but this time there was a surgical saw in a plastic bag, lying on the ground under her body, drenched in blood. Inside the plastic bag, all looked over at each other and back at Donovan. Alice and the tech placed the young girl on the gurney, and Donovan and the others moved in closer. Scott snapped a few pictures as Donovan picks up the bag, by the handle gracefully and hands it to Stein for McKnight, "Get this to Mac and see if we have prints?"

Scott snapped a few more pictures of the ground and then moved over to the headstone. Donovan looked around more, scanning the scene, taking a hard look at the headstone, and then returned to the SUV, followed by O'Malley and MacBride.

"Who called it in?' MacBride asked.

"The night watchman," O'Malley said, pointing over at the uniformed guard—black pants, white dress shirt, and black hat and tie —well into his sixties, near one of the patrol cars in front of O'Malley's SUV.

"Tell them again, what you told my partner," O'Malley said.

The old man still leaning on the car, wiping his mouth after vomiting, "I was doing my rounds, saw something or someone lying over there by the tombstone, thought it was kids screwin'. We have had them before and have caught many lately, both boys and girls, and just girls, but when I walked up to them, I could tell it was three girls. I called out and told them to leave, but they didn't move. I flashed my light on them and saw those eyes, those cold dead eyes, the missing hands, and then I ran. I read about the ones in the newspapers, you'll find in the forest, and called you guys." He explained, wiping his mouth again and standing up straight.

Donovan moved back to the SUV. Stein had now returned; O'Malley and MacBride followed. "Three more tonight, isn't that odd?" Stein asked. "Thought it was one at a time, that's how the forest was."

"The suspect is getting bold, or desperate," Donovan explained, looking at O'Malley. "Now that Camille has put it out there. The suspect loves the fanfare." He looked around at the small group gathering behind the tapeline. "Fanfare?" Stein asked.

"Serial killers love the show. They love being the center of attention, some even work themselves into a case. Now that Camille has reported the bodies, the suspect will escalate and will be looking for the press, more attention by way of the girls. Match these to the missing and deceased, which should be the most recent ones, and let me know if there are any more current ones still missing." Donovan explained.

MacBride and Stein nodded in agreement, and O'Malley let out a heavy sigh. Like Donovan, he did not like the press either, or did not wish to talk with Camille, but knew he would have to.

"Meet you both back at the Station, T?" O'Malley said as he stepped up and into the SUV and Stein moved around to the other side.

"In a bit, I'm going to meet someone, first," Donovan said, as O'Malley waved back and drove off.

"Who are we going to meet?" MacBride asked climbing back into her car. "Not meet, just look in on. I want to drive up to the old Sherman Estate."

MacBride drove slowly through the open gates of the Sherman Estates, a high arching metal gate, with 'SHERMAN," along the archway at the top, and around the long circular driveway up to the Sherman house. A large fountain sat near the house in the round, two cherubs kissing, and peeing into the fountain, but their penises have removed, with only a slit for the water to exit through.

MacBride was shocked upon seeing it but also disgusted by it.

Lights were on in one of the upstairs bedrooms above the living room and the living room on the right side of the house. They could tell two were in the bedroom, upstairs, by figures moving around, and then one standing and jumping from time to time.

Donovan rolled down his window and heard a smacking noise, then, "Thank you, Ma'am. May I have another?" His eyes narrowed as the car came to a stop, he continued to watch the upstairs window.

He motioned to MacBride to stay back in the car, as he climbed out and walked up the oversized porch and stairs. Two wicker chairs and a table sat off to his right, and a wicker swing chair off to his left, dirty and dusty, he could tell the porch had not been used in years. The estate was old, over two hundred years old, one of the oldest Estates in town, and he slowly looked into the first-floor window. He saw an old woman in her wheelchair near the fireplace, nude, age had not treated her well for her eighties, and then he heard another smack. "Thank you Ma'am. May I have another?" He glanced up, "and whose a good little girl," another woman said, he chuckled, and then looked back inside, a woman in her forties entered the living room, with only her white nurse's hat, white stockings, and white nursing shoes. "Is this better Ma'am?" Dancing naked for the old woman, turned around, pushing her ass out, the old woman squeezing it and fondling it. In a low and groggy voice, the old woman says, "Yes baby, yes, shake it like momma likes it."

Donovan shook his head slowly, and returned down the steps, hearing another smack from upstairs, "Thank you, Ma'am? May I have another?"

"Good girl, who's my good girl?" the other woman asked.

"What did you see?" MacBride asked as he opened the door.

"One old kinky bitch fondling her nurse's ass," he said locking his seatbelt in place.

"And what was that from upstairs?" MacBride asked with her eyes wide open from his comment.

"A woman getting whipped by another woman, from the two female voices, most likely, and asking for more," he answered waving her to drive off.

"Yea, that's one kinky old bitch."

"And family, I believe Old Lady Sherman and Daughter are into BDSM with other women. Not sure yet how it relates to the case or just a coincidence that the bodies were in Sherman's Forest and the new ones tonight in the cemetery. I am starting to think someone is trying to tell me something," Donovan said as if talking to himself, and looking back through the side mirror.

"You don't believe in coincidences," She said looking back in the rear-view mirror as they exit the gate of the Estate.

"True,"

Interviews

The bright morning Sun blinded Donovan as he exited his trailer and entered the Roadhouse. Wearing black jeans, a black t-shirt, and boots, with his shield and SIG on his waistband. Jock was cleaning glasses, wearing a grey t-shirt and his old white cap, and Donovan sat at the bar. "Jock, Sarah had told me a while back that your family has been in Jackson Hole about as long as the Shermans, and mine. What can you tell me about them before my time?"

Jock let out a heavy sigh and tossed the wash towel on his shoulder. "That's a long story and a bizarre one. There are rumors in the windows. My Father told me a story once when I was a teenager after I saw something out there. Promise me you will not tell Sarah and the girls," Donovan nodded. Jock pulled out two small glasses and poured some whiskey. "Except for a few notable males, with military distinction. The women have been very close, and I mean *very* close," staring right at him, "A friend and I once cut across their property, after fishing at Indian Lake to get home quickly when I was eleven or twelve. We were running through the woods and came upon Old Lady Sherman, the one in the wheelchair now. She was about thirty, maybe forty then, and she was nude, as were two young daughters, a little younger than me and my friend. They were kissing and fondling each other, between their legs and around their breasts. We watched from the bushes, as boys do, and it opened our eyes. The girls were calling their mom 'Ma'am,' and she was calling them 'my little plaything'."

Donovan grabbed the glass of whisky and drank it down fast. "That answers a few questions about what I heard and saw last night, and rumors growing up. Old Lady Sherman was seriously fondling one of her nurse's asses while the nurse was naked with only her cap, stockings, and shoes, dancing around, and from upstairs, I kept hearing a woman saying, 'Yes, Ma'am. May I have another?' And another woman telling her she was a good girl."

"I believe the daughter was upstairs receiving them from another woman or nurse," Jock said, pouring him some more whiskey.

"What story did your Father tell you?" Donovan asked, looking back at him, contemplating taking another drink.

"When I got home after she yelled some very profound words at me and my friend, I told him I thought I was going to get my ass beaten for lying, making up the story of what I saw, and cutting across their land. He told me, 'That old woman was crazy. All the women enjoy sex with one another, and the young ones were always submissive. I have also heard she had some very kinky female parties up there,'" Jock said, sipping at his glass.

"So, the Sherman women have a very dark side? What do you know about the Granddaughter that ran away?"

Jock took a couple of seconds and thought, sniffing his whiskey. "I heard from a lady once who was a nurse there that they used to really beat her and abuse her sexually."

"Who was the Nurse?"

"Ms. Clair Davendish, the ER charge nurse at the Hospital, back then."

"How long ago was this?" Donovan asked as he took a sip.

"I think, Sarah was about fifteen then, the Granddaughter was coming in the ER because of abuse, but the hospital put it down as she was a klutz and accident-prone. The Granddaughter would be in her late twenties now, maybe thirties, I think."

"Why did she come to you, about this?" Donovan asked sipping some more.

"Not me. She came over one night to talk with Rebecca, Sarah's Mother, she was very distraught and scared. Old Lady Sherman had come into the hospital and was very demanding, regarding her Granddaughter's treatment, flirting with the female staff, and slapping young girls' asses. Rebecca was a social worker, remember?" Donovan nods, "wanting to know what she could do with this old bat as she put it. I heard them talking, I went into the kitchen and told my story. Rebecca was horrified."

"For you not telling her what you knew, or?" Donovan asked, not wanting to know the answer.

"She couldn't handle it, was very religious, and could not believe that stuff happened between women, and told Ms. Davendish to leave. She could not believe a Mother would do what I said I saw her doing with her daughters. We never spoke of it again," Jock paused, sipped from his glass of whiskey, and leaned back on the counter behind him, and then it hit him. "Those bodies you'll found, were they, in Sherman's forest? The families' old land, you think they are connected?"

Donovan started to answer, but MacBride walked in, and saw the glasses on the bar, "thought you didn't drink when on the job?"

"I thought he needed it with all that was going on," Jock said, trying to help. "Don't feed his addictions, Dad. You have done enough of that by letting him win the bar in the poker game. We got the reports from the Forensic Anthropologist," she said as she dropped a stack of folders on the bar in front of him.

"Was O'Malley right, up to about a month?"

"Yes, the first killing was a month ago and very sloppy, the Anthropologist stated in her report that blunt force trauma was the cause. Dr. Beyer believes she hit her head on a stone surface and hard."

"The base of a fireplace step?" Donovan commented as he remembered the fireplace in the Sherman's house. "He did not say anything of where, but it could be. Why?"

"I saw one in the Sherman's house last night when I took my stroll," Donovan replied opening the top folder.

"That old bat is crazy," MacBride said throwing her arms up, Jock and Donovan looked at each other, both thinking, like Mother, like Daughter.

"Thanks for the drinks, Jock, back to work," Donovan said standing, winking, and grabbing the files, each man just looking at the other, Jock nodded.

MacBride drove and Donovan looked over the files, "Dr. Beyer states each one had their legs and wrist bound anti-mortem, and all were very dehydrated."

"Kept for a time?" MacBride asked glancing over and back on the road quickly. He skimmed two more folders, "Yes, but not the same head trauma. So, the earliest may have been the first kill."

"Could she tell how long the bodies were held?" she asked as she pulled into her parking stall, which had her name, 'Captain S. MacBride,' painted on the ground near the rear of the stall. He collected the folders, got out, and they both entered the station. They notice a forest ranger in the conference room, Stein joined them near his office, "O'Malley brought him in, and just left, said you would know what to do with him."

He handed the folders back to MacBride and took the one Stein had, "Shall we," he said, holding the folder out and directing Stein, "See if Scott's team can match these reports to the missing persons," Donovan asked, MacBride nodded.

They walked into the room, "This is Lieutenant Donavan, he is the lead detective on the case, he has some more questions for you," Stein said as they sat down across from the ranger. The man was white in his late forties, wearing khakis slacks and a shirt. His ranger hat is on the desk, a normal Smokey the Bear type, and his name badge states, R. Stevenson."

"Ranger Stevenson, I just have a few questions for you," Donovan repeated.

"Rick," he replied.

Stein and Donovan looked at each other with shit-eating grins, 'Ranger Rick,' she said as he opened the folder, and skimmed a section, "You had told Detective O'Malley, you had been in the area about three hours prior and also that you needed to finish your rounds. I know Sherman's forest is a good size, but you should have been able to cover it within three hours and been done by the time O'Malley found you. You stated you did not see anything when you started your shift?"

Ranger Rick squirmed in his chair, "I was unable to start my rounds because we have been having problems with an old army vet who has become a hermit in the woods, I saw him in the area where you all found the girls, but as soon as I saw him, he took off."

Duke knocked on the door and handed Donovan a piece of page. He skimmed it, nodded, and sat back down, placing the paper under the folders, Stein tried to see, "How long have you been working for the Ranger service?"

"About five years." the Ranger said quickly, squirming more in his chair.

"Then how can we have over half a dozen bodies from a month ago till yesterday, and you have seen nothing?"

"Just didn't." the Ranger said, cautiously.

"Ok, do you know the name of the hermit?" Stein asked, leaning forward some. Ranger Rick paused for a moment, looking at each of them, then back at Donovan, "Captain Walker Grant, Army Medical Corps, I think."

Stein copied the name down on a pad she had. "A Doctor?"

"I believe so."

"We'll check that out, so what happened between the times you spotted him and returned to find O'Malley and the rest of the department at the scene?" Donovan asked patiently.

The Ranger twisted his hat some, thinking, stalling, "I ran after him for about a mile and lost him along the cliff line. He Rambo'd me and jumped off the cliff."

"You're, what," he said looking him over, sizing him up, "about six feet tall, and could run for about … let's say two, three miles, an hour or so," he nodded, and Donovan continued," so what did you do for about the last two hours, before returning?"

He squirmed more; Donovan knew he was hiding something.

"I got lost out there in the dark."

Stein and Donovan looked at each other, having a hard time believing this. "You have been a Ranger in the park for five years, mostly at night, and you got lost," Donovan said quickly, then slammed his hand on the desk, "What happened!"

Ranger Rick bit his nails on his right hand. "I ran after that hermit, he Rambo'd me, and I got lost in the area."

"What is your supervisor's name?" Donovan asked, staring straight at him, and waiting.

"Lawyer?"

Donovan stormed out; Stein followed, and closed the door behind them, "Why did you quiet?"

"He Lawyered up," Donovan said still looking over the Ranger's

file. "I've heard that never stopped you before."

"There is too much with this case, I don't wish to miss a step and have to back up or have a DA railroading me," Donovan said, as he placed the paper Duke gave him in the folder, signed it with his left hand, and closed the file.

"But...."

MacBride stepped up, "How's it going?"

"He Lawyer'd up and your ace detective here just walked out," Stein said raising her voice some. MacBride looked at Donovan, and then at Stein, "It's his case." Donovan continued off to his office, Stein rolled her eyes and returned to her desk.

MacBride followed Donovan to his office and saw their daughter Marci was sitting on the couch with a redhead like Mother's but dyed dark black, very Goth, sixteen, wearing a black skirt, black leggings, black heels, and a black hoodie, black lipstick, and heavy black eyeliner. Donovan casually glanced at Marci as he walked in, he was not happy with how she was dressed, and with all her makeup, but let it go.

"Marci, I asked you to cut back on the makeup," MacBride said following him in and was appalled at her look.

"Mom!" Marci answered, huffing and smacking her gum.

"Don't Mom me, young lady," MacBride replied very sternly.

Letting out a heavy sigh, not looking at her Mom, she swung her legs up in haste, and walked over to Donovan's desk, dropping her hoodie onto her shoulders. Takes it off and lays it on a chair, she has a grey T-shirt on, with white lettering, and with a large pink heart. MacBride pulled her shirt down to see it better, it stated, 'I heart pussy."

"What the hell is this?" MacBride yells with shock, looking at Donovan and then back at Marci."Sarah!" Donovan said, cutting her off and looking up from reading some mail that was on his desk.

"Pointing at her shirt, "You see this? What is this?" she said, looking at Donovan first then pointing to Marci."

"It's a shirt, Mom," Marci replied very sarcastically.

"My Daughter does not wear stuff like this; you agree Donovan?" MacBride said he was now reading a new folder, "Donovan!" she yelled and he looked up, and over at the shirt, which she is still holding to show him as if evidence.

Donovan looked it over thoroughly and then back at MacBride, "She's sixteen, let her be, it's cute."

"Cute, let her be, *my* Daughter does not wear shit like this!" MacBride yelled. Marci grabbed her hoodie and ran out. "Now, see what you did?"

Putting the folder down, "I think you're overreacted Sarah, it's just a shirt."

"How could you not side with me?" MacBride asked looking right at him.

"Side with you? She is also my daughter, she is growing up, give her time, it may be just a fad." Donovan said sitting down.

"The Psychologist had spoken," MacBride yelled storming out almost hitting Stein, who was coming in.

"Everything ok?" Stein asked looking back at MacBride.

"Mom is having an issue with *our* Daughter's outfit."

Stein looked back, having seen the shirt, and smiling, and hoping he did not see her look, "Give her time, she'll come around." Stein said.

"What you got?" he asked, seeing the folder in her hand.

He opened it and read, "Captain Walker Grant, U. S. Army medical corps, and his specialty is Orthopedics, hands predominately." Stein said then handed him the folder.

He looked at her, and took the folder, "Is this his whole record, taking a single page out of the folder?"

"No, a preliminary. I got that off the internet. I called a contact I have in the Army, and she will fax me his full record in a day or so." Stein answered.

"Good," Donovan said taking a photo of Grant from the folder that was a single page, white, thirty-three, brown hair, and clean shaven, in uniform, and he taped it on the whiteboard under, 'Left hands cut off like a surgeon,' and then turned back toward Stein, "Find out who Ranger Rick's supervisor is, and his normal schedule, please. I want more on him before his lawyer shows up."

"Yes, but still think you should have drilled him," Stein said sternly.

"Go!" Donovan ordered looking over the board, not looking at her.

His desk phone rang, "Donovan … yes, OK, bring her in O'Malley." he put the phone back down, "Stein!"

She returned quickly, "Yes,"

"O'Malley has found an eyewitness that was jogging the morning the dog found the hand. Said she saw a figure in the area where the dog and fisherman had found the body. He is bringing her in, find the sketch artist, please," Donovan explained, Stein nodded and left.

MacBride stepped in, "Did I hear you right, O'Malley has a witness?" Donovan nodded.

O'Malley and Stein were in the conference room with a female sketch artist, with dark hair, a young female, wearing a deputy's uniform, and a young woman in her thirties, jeans, and a blue blouse. Donovan and MacBride joined them, "This is Mrs. North, she was jogging arly that that morning at sunrise, and saw a figure in the forest, moving slowly and carrying something heavy," O'Malley said.

"How good of a look did you get, Mrs. North?" Donovan asked.

"Could you tell if it was a man or woman?" MacBride asked.

"Body size was not too large but no I could not tell." Mrs. North said as she looked at Donovan.

"Anything else you can tell us," Stein asked.

"I did hear a large vehicle, like a truck or van revving up before the figure left the area," Mrs. North answered looking from Stein to Donovan.

Donovan shook her hand and handed her one of his business cards, "If you remember anything else, please don't hesitate to call, anytime," Donovan said.

"I will show you out," Stein said showing her the way out toward the front entrance.

"What you get Maggie?" O'Malley asked. She held up the sketch, it was just a medium-sized figure wearing a black outfit, hoodie, and no face, but had a bag, like a medical bag.

"Ask the Fisherman again if he heard the truck or van, O'Malley?" Donovan asked. O'Malley left and Maggie tore the page off the pad and followed him out. MacBride turned the page around on the table. "That was a complete waste of time," Stein commented as she returned, Donovan looked at MacBride and left.

"You need to start working with us, or I will reassign you back to traffic," MacBride said knowing it was a trying time for all of them.

"If you are not charging my client, then we're leaving," A young man in his thirties, looking like he was right out of high school, in a nice three-piece gray suit, sat behind the table in the interrogation room with Ranger Rick, as Donovan and Stein entered.

"We only have a couple of questions to verify your client's whereabouts, after he started his shift and when Detective O'Malley interviewed him, he is the only eyewitness at this point, but if he does not answer my questions. I will arrest him and hold him for forty-eight hours, which I can do, for obstruction." Donovan said he sat and opened the folder he had with him.

"And I will slap you with a false arrest charge," the young lawyer said, taking a legal pad out and closing his briefcase, placing it on the floor.

"Then just answer my questions, I don't think he is a suspect, I am only trying to put together a timeline, and then he can leave," Donovan said, looking at the ranger and then the Lawyer.

"No strings?" the Lawyer asked.

"No strings," Donovan replied, looking over the file again.

The young Lawyer leaned over to Ranger Rick and whispered in his ear, and then Ranger Rick whispered back, "If any information he gives does not pertain to *your* case, he can leave?"

"If it does not pertain to *my* case, yes, he can leave," Donovan said with his right hand up as if swearing on a bible.

They whispered again, and the Lawyer shakes his head no, "Ask your first Question."

"Why did it take you two hours to return to the site and finish your shift, being lost is not an answer," Donovan asked looking directly at Ranger Rick.

They whispered again, and the Lawyer waved his hand in front of Ranger Rick to answer, "I have a pot farm up in the woods and was tending it."

Stein pulled a map of the area out of the folder she had, "Where?"

Ranger Rick opened the map, took the pen from her, and circled an area, she handed it to Donovan, and he started for the door.

"It does not pertain to *the* case, right?" the Lawyer asked.

"No, it did not pertain to *my* case, but I never said anything about the DEA," Donovan said as he opened the door and two DEA Agents, an African American man in his late fifties, and a blonde woman in her twenties, both with lanyards and windbreakers with "DEA," on their backs, wait. "All yours, Stan," Donovan said to the older man as if they know each other, and they walked in, the blonde cuffed Ranger Rick, and Stan read him his rights. Donovan closed the door behind him, leaving with Stein.

"How the fuck did you know that," Stein asked, in the hallway with O'Malley, who has now joined them. "Remember the note Duke handed me in the first interview?" Donovan said looking from her then O'Malley.

"Yes," Stein said, as Donovan walked off, she turned fast to O'Malley. "He'll grow on ya," O'Malley said with a shit-eating grin.

Donovan walked into MacBride's office with the folder and map, "The DEA will need this once they're done and you sign off, we have Ranger Rick on drug possession and growing, and I have turned him over."

"Good Job,"

Donovan walked back into his office and opened another folder on his desk, Duke entered, "Good to have you back, Nephew."

"Yeah, you got something?" he said without looking up.

"Just checking on you, Nephew, been a while since we talked."

He looked up, "Yes, been hard since the divorce, not wishing to talk or see anyone. Lucky, I had the grill, kept has me busy," he answered as he walked over to Duke, "You and Auntie have been a big help recently and back then when Dad and Mom passed." They hugged, and Duke looked as if hiding something.

Stein knocked on the door, and both men separated, she opened the door. "O'Malley has a woman you need to talk to. She was at the cemetery the same night as the night watchman."

"This is Mrs. Reilly. She was leaving the cemetery when a van matching the description Mrs. North gave was seen," O'Malley said as he sat next to Mrs. Reilly, a woman in her late forties with brownish-red hair, wearing a blue dress, sitting at the end of the long conference table. Donovan and Stein entered.

"Yes, O'Malley?" Donovan asked as he and Stein sat near them.

"Please tell Lieutenant Donovan, what you told me, Mrs. Reilly, please."

"I was leaving my Father's grave, down the road from the Sherman's plot. A tan or light brown van nearly ran me off the road. At first, I just drove on, but then something told me to go back, and we should exchange insurance." She said looking at Donovan and hoping not to get in trouble for leaving the scene of an accident.

Donovan nodded. "No worries, we are more concerned with the van. Please go on."

"I stopped near the Van and walked up the path. It was dark, and two people were dragging something. Not sure what they were dragging, but it was heavy."

"Could you see or tell anything more about the two dragging the bodies?" "I heard a voice and could tell it was a man and a woman. She was the leader, she was commanding him, and he did not want to be there."

Donovan looked over at O'Malley. "How many bodies did you see being dragged?" Donovan asked.

"They were both dragging one each. Then when they got back to the Van, I saw the smaller one, the man I think, pulling another out and dropping it. I slipped and thought they heard me and left."

"Thank you," Donovan said as he handed her a business card. "She document it all?"

"No, but I will have her before she leaves," O'Malley said.

Donovan entered a large storage room filled with many shelf units, rummaging for something. Opened a box and pulled out two old brown folders. The box was labeled, 'Lt. Donovan, Malachi A.' with handwriting on the front. He opened one, reads, and is very confused. "DUI, funny Duke never told me that," and opens the second one. "This does not add up. First, they reported a fire, then they had to physically cut the front windshield out."

Donovan could not believe what he was reading. Duke had always told him the truth: his Father hit the tree after swerving from a deer. But its states here that he was shot off the road. "What is Duke hiding?" Donovan also read his last case was with the Shermans.

The Pearl Drop Club

Donovan and Stein stood opposite Roberts in the morgue. The first girl found in the forest was lying on the table with only her head showing, her body covered by a white sheet. Roberts was now in blue scrubs and gloves, Donovan and Stein were also wearing gloves.

"Female, sixteen. Death by strangulation due to asphyxiation, ligature marks on the remaining wrist and ankles, as well as the hand found at the scene," Roberts pulled the sheet down to show the girl's naked body. "As you can see, there are red and purple bruising along her abdomen, legs, and inner thighs, and virginal area," Roberts reported, as she pointed over the girl's body.

"Raped?" Stein asked.

"Both orifices, but I don't believe it was done by a male unless we have a male that is at least five inches thick around in town."

"Any semen?" Stein asked.

"No, but. . . "

"But. . . " Donovan said.

"She had both virginal and anal intercourse before death and after. I can tell from the bruising and some tearing, but non-consensual, from the intensity of the bruising. Help me roll her over, please?" Roberts asked as the three slowly turned the body over onto her belly. Donovan and Stein looked at each other questioningly, then back at Roberts. "Yes, all bodies have this tattoo along their backs."

A large tramp stamp on her lower back, "MOMMY'S PLAYTHING," scrolled on her lower back in curving arches, magnificently in green and black ink, with two crosses, one under the word 'Mommy's and the other under the word 'Plaything,' curlicues and twists, a very professional job.

"Maybe she was into girls, and her boyfriend could not take it," Stein said and believed a man had done it.

"Not a man. The bruising was intense around the anus, the bruising was stiff, and not from a penis from the size of the opening. I found no trace of epidermal flaking as I would with a typical female rape case. No offense, Donovan."

"None was taken," Donovan said as he looked up from the tattoo again.

"With what then?" Stein asked.

Alice walked towards her desk at the far end of the room, took one of her gloves off, and took her purse out of one of the larger drawers. It was a large oversized brown purse with gold metal chains around the hand straps. She laid it on top of one of the empty tables. "This," she said as she pulled out an eight-inch by four-inch-thick dildo in a harness." Donovan and Stein looked down. "Don't worry, this one's mine."

Stein licked her lips and winked at Roberts, who winked back. "Hmm, nice Strappy?" she said as she reached for it.

"Shall I give you ladies the room?" Donovan said as he turned towards the door.

"One more thing," Roberts said as she stopped him. "I found this in her panties, they all had them," Roberts explained as she handed him a small business card.

He read it and looked back at Stein and then Roberts. "The Pearl Drop Club, our next stop."

"Donovan," Roberts said, clearing her throat, pausing, and then looking back at Stein. "That's a ladies-only fetish club. Men are not allowed."

Stein stepped up near Roberts. "A cougar and kitty cat club?"

"Yes, I know the type of club it is, but Ms. Amanda will see me," Donovan said, looking up from the card at both of them.

"You know the owner?" Roberts asked, with surprised.

"I gave her and my sister, Annabelle, the seed money to help them out of bankruptcy eight years ago. When Annabelle passed two years ago, she willed the club to me. Ms. Amanda and I are good friends and partners."

Both women looked at each other confused, never heard of a man associated with the club.

It was a very plain building in the warehouse district, with two red doors seated along the brown wall, a white and orange neon sign on the roof, a small white minx kitten wearing a teardrop pearl necklace and resting against a martini glass. The sign read "Pearl Drop Club" in yellow and pink neon lights.

Two women, one with red hair and the other blonde, dressed in very short black skirts, white blouses, long black men's ties, knee-high black boots, and each wearing heavy red lipstick and black eyeliner. About ten other women were waiting to enter, in a little black dress, and different outfits for different bondage role-playing scenarios. Their ages range each ranging from early twenties to late fifties. A large African American woman in her forties sat on a stool near the door, a bodybuilder in a red tracksuit. The redhead puts her hand up to Donovan as he and MacBride approach the red velvet rope at the front of the line. "Oh no, this is a ladies-only club. Your sweetheart is very welcome," she said as she looked MacBride over, "but you, no,"

"Rachel, you know me, now please advise, Ms. Amanda, I will be at the back door." Rachel laughed as she recognized him and looked back at the blonde, who also laughed and stepped over toward Donovan. "Tell Ms. Amanda that her partner is here and he will be at the back door," Rachel said as she waved toward the blonde, who stepped inside.

Ms. Amanda, blonde in her mid-thirties, long black dress, very tight to her body, and heels, sat at a small round table in a sea of tables along each side of a large ballroom with a young girl, about eighteen. The girl was wearing a white ball gown with a teardrop pearl necklace and long white gloves. The blonde woman from outside leaned down and whispered into Ms. Amanda's ear, "Donovan is out back, said he was your partner and would meet you at the back door."

"Crap!" Amanda said under her breath and leaned over and caressed her companion under her chin. "Mommy will be back in a bit," Amanda kissed her on her lips a few times, then stood, and the girl smiled innocently. Amanda followed the blonde toward the back entrance.

Amanda pushed the emergency door open without the alarm sounding. Donovan caught it, and MacBride stood next to him. "Donovan, we had an agreement?"

"You've heard of the murders?"

"Yes, those poor girls."

"Those poor girls were dressed in black and white ball gowns, with teardrop pearl necklaces, and we found the club's business cards on them. I need to search and question your staff," Donovan said, starting to step inside.

Amanda sighed. A mature woman in her late forties walked up from behind Amanda, with brown hair, stark naked except for a large, long thick strap-on, and it was swinging in front of her as she walked up. Her large breast sagged, and she placed a hand on Amanda's shoulder. Sara's eyes widened. "Ms. Amanda, I had requested a young girl for tonight, not one my age." Then she saw Donovan. "Oh, Hey Donovan?"

"Hello Mayor Whitefield. I see you are about to have a nice evening," Donovan said, then she realized he was there. "Don't worry, Ms. Whitefield. What happens in the club stays in the club."

Amanda turned slightly to her right. "Robin, please assist Mistress Catherine with her requests, my pet?" Robin nodded slightly toward the Mayor. "Mistress Catherine, please follow me?" Robin asked with her hand stretched out.

"I need to question a few of the girls and women, as well as staff of your Debutante ball, and maybe others, in private. Afterward, I wish to survey the ballroom from the office," Donovan explained.

"Fine, Donovan," Amanda said, not wanting him there and knowing he was the senior partner who could cause trouble, and turned, and walked back the way she came. They followed the door slammed closed, and they continued back down the brick hallway. Amanda turned left, and the walls changed to a nice brown paneling, a larger hallway with doors on both sides, like a hotel. They passed a room, numbered eight, with a young girl, in a Princess-style room, looking more like a pre-teen than in her twenties, with a four-poster bed, white dresser, Hello Kitty bedspread, and a large Hello Kitty doll on an oversized chair. The Mayor walked up from across the room ahead of Donovan, smiling, then entered the room. The young girl, naked except for a diaper, puffy young breasts, a pacifier, and blonde pigtails waiting patiently, kneeling on the bed. She took her pacifier out. "Mommy!" she called out, jumping up and down on the bed in excitement. The Major stepped into the room. "Are you my plaything tonight?" the Major asked, then turned back toward Donovan. Her tone changed to a more commanding voice. "Or my bitch!" she stated as she closed the door in front of him, with the girl still excited at seeing her Mommy.

"This way," Amanda said, and they continued down the hallway. A young girl turned the corner in front of them. She was in her twenties, with red hair and dressed in a yellow and white cheer leading outfit, short skirt, pompoms, and a large black "B" on her large chest. She ran up to MacBride, jumped up, and grabbed her in a big hug, with arms and legs around her. "Mommy, it's been so long."

Donovan looked at MacBride. MacBride was a bit shocked, thinking he might be angry like most men are, but he said with a smile, "Go ahead, Mommy, and have fun with your little cheerleader. I've got this," Donovan said.

MacBride looked back at the girl, and then at Donovan, he waved them off, and they ran off, skipping and holding hands as if they were young schoolgirls.

"Room twelve is open," Ms. Amanda yelled down the hallway.

"You didn't know? You knew she was a member?" Amanda asked.

"Annabelle told me shortly before her death," Donovan said, putting his hand out for Ms. Amanda to continue.

Amanda's office was large, but more like a cheap and corrupted Lawyer's, one with fake oak wood paneling and very ornate, a large oak desk on the far end to their right, twin chairs, and a couch set near the wall to their left, black leather, and red lush carpet. They entered from the far end near the oversized fireplace, and there was a large oversized portrait of Ms. Annabelle with long flowing red hair, dark olive skin, and bright green eyes. She was wearing a white wrap, the door closed back into the wall as a hidden door. There was an overside window on his left behind the desk with long red curtains.

"Care for a drink? Oh, that's right, you don't drink on the job," Amanda said, but Donovan just cleared his throat. She would move, she put the vase and glasses down, walked to the curtains, and flung them open more, revealing the ballroom. "Don't worry, it's a one-way mirror behind the bar. Annabelle always loved this view."

The window opened onto a large ballroom with three bartenders, all wearing blue or red bikinis behind the bar, young girls dressed either in white or black ball gowns with long white gloves. Donovan then noticed that each of the victims did not have the gloves, but they all had with teardrop pearl necklaces. The women ranged between sixteen to twenty-five. The women ranged from mid-thirties to early sixties, mostly thirties and forties, wearing long black dresses, some with stockings and jewelry, and looked very high class in appearance. A few of the girls were at the bar along with a few ladies sipping drinks. The servers were dressed like the two girls out front. There were ten to fifteen women and girls dancing out on the dance floor to music, which they could not hear inside the office. Donovan could tell that the mature ladies were leading. A few other couples were at tables as Amanda was earlier, chatting or kissing their dates, and a few couples in the back were going at it. "Just a minute?" Amanda turned back to her desk, picked up the phone, and pressed a single button, and one of the bartenders at the right of the bar, which Donovan could see, answered, "Please move the ladies in the back to a private room, please."

The bartender flagged down Robin, who was now back working the room. He watched as the bartender motioned to her and the three couples in the back, who were going at it, fondling, and kissing lower on the girls, lower than their necks. Robin walked to the back and talked to each couple, leading them off through a door to their right.

"I see you're still keeping the good stuff in private rooms," Donovan commented.

They continued to watch as a lady in her late forties ran in, up to a couple on the dance floor. She pushed the mature lady aside and backhanded the young girl, causing her to fall back hard onto the floor.

The lady she pushed, pushed her back, Amanda pressed a button on the ledge near the window. Donovan watched as those on the dance floor stopped and continued watching the catfight.

Five servers moved in with Robin, pulling them apart and helped the younger girl up. Amanda pushed another button next to the first. "Remove Ms. Davendish to the cell and take Ms. Cooper and her date to the infirmary," Donovan looked over at Amanda and then back at Ms. Davendish, a name he remembered from the talk he had with Jock early that morning.

"The Cell?"

"Yes, a place we put the more disruptive ones, for a time, and a private place for you to talk. This is not the first time she has done this, a couple of times before, and she has put a few girls in the hospital."

Donovan looked at her. "How long has Ms. Davendish been a member?" Donovan asked, watching Robin and the other servers escort her and the couple off the dance floor, out through the main lobby, through the door below where he was standing, behind the bar.

"Two years. She was a guest of the Mayor, but now the Mayor wants nothing to do with her anymore."

"And what happens in the cell?"

"As I said, a disciplinary room, but you will have a chair, and she will be naked. The cell is for punishment, but I feel after what she just did, it is private enough for you and a few others you wish to talk to," Amanda said, looking sideways at him.

He nodded and noticed the ladies dancing again and one lonely-looking girl at one of the tables, and knowing she was Amanda's type. "I hope I am not keeping you from your date. She seems lonely."

"Yes," Amanda pushed another button on her desk. Another woman in her early thirties, dressed in a white tuxedo with a white bow tie, bodybuilder, and long brunette hair, entered. He noticed some amount of white powder on her hands. "Give Lieutenant Donovan any help he needs." The woman looked him over, knowing no men were allowed in the club, then at Amanda. "He is Ms. Annabelle's Brother and my senior partner," she nodded.

"Thank you, Ms. Amanda. I will try not to disturb your clients."

"I loved Ms. Annabelle very much, and I know you did too. You were the one who gave her the money for this place, so make yourself at home. Ms. Annabelle would not have it any other way. Jacqueline, here, we'll help you," Amanda said, leaving.

Donovan looked back out into the ballroom. Jacqueline stepped up next to him. "We all loved Ms. Annabelle. She was an Angel," Jacqueline said, holding back some tears.

"Thank you. I hope I am wrong for her sake, but so far all leads, lead here. I will also need to talk to the bartenders, the woman Ms. Davendish assaulted, and her date. As well as any girls that she has had issues with, and the rest of the staff."

"Yes… Sir."

"It's ok. I know the staff and others have been trained to say 'Ma'am,' 'Mommy,' or 'Miss.' Donovan or T will be fine."

"Yes, Donovan."

"Who is that sitting three tables past Ms. Amanda? She looks familiar," Donovan asked, watching as Amanda returned to her table, kissing her date.

Jacqueline shifted from his left side to his right for a better look. "That's U.S. Senator Murphy. She comes in whenever she is in town." Senator Murphy was in her late fifties and sat with two young girls, both in white dresses and teardrop pearl necklaces. A server placed three long-stemmed glasses with champagne down on the table. All three sipped, giggled, and stood exiting through the backdoor, which Robin had taken the couples out earlier. Both girls were holding onto the Senator. "Will you need to talk with her?"

"No, like the Mayor, I will let them enjoy their playthings."

She nodded and saw him looking at a young blonde at the table on the far side of the room, mid-twenties white ball gown, with a lady in her sixties, very elegant and lovely looking, and sat down, "You know her?" Jacquelyn asked.

"No," Donovan said. She reminded me of the young girls in the forest.

"Wish to talk to her too?"

"No, how long has she been here?"

Jacquelyn thought, "About two months, very quiet before that."

"The young girl reminds me of the girls we found in the forest," Donovan explained.

Jacqueline swallowed, Donovan saw some sweat trickling down her face, and felt her nervousness, "Should I arrange for you to talk with the lady and young girl, too?"

"No, just any personal and company information you have. Let's go talk with Ms. Davendish, now."

Donovan waited behind the wheel of MacBride's sedan, with his arm out the window adjusting the mirror. MacBride quickly ran out of the club and climbed into the passenger's side, and fell in, without her jacket, her blouse inside out, and hanging out. A couple of buttons were missing as if ripped off, and her bra was hanging from her back pocket. The makeup she did have on earlier was a mess from the sweat on her face, and lipstick marks on her cheeks and neck.

"Mommy had a good time with her little girl?" Donovan asked, trying not to laugh.

"How did you know? This was not the reason I divorced you."

"You divorced me because of the long hours we had to work, and you said you could not live with me anymore. What you wish to do in private is not my concern, but I do hope you had fun," Donovan said, adjusting the rear-view mirror and sitting up.

Her smile turned to a half frown. "How did you learn of this place as a leader?

"This afternoon, Stein and I were with Alice Roberts, as she was telling us that the girls all had intercourse before death, no semen, but consensual sex, virginally and anally forced. The way each girl was dressed reminded me of the club, and each girl had a tramp stamp, 'Mommy's Plaything,' on their lower backs." Donovan said looking around.

"How did you deduce it was a woman, and this place?" MacBride asked, re-buttoning her shirt quickly and fixing her hair.

"Not sure if it's one of the women here yet, just a few leads led us here. Dana asked how, and Alice commented, no seam or epidurals, and large scarring, about four to five inches in the openings, took out her strap-on, and they both smiled and winked. I offered to give them the room. Alice stopped me and showed me this," Donovan explained, handing her the business card that Roberts gave him from his inside coat pocket, now in an evidence bag. She took it and read it.

"What else did you learn in there?" She asked, pulling the rear-view mirror toward her, putting herself back together the best she could.

"Well, you were having yourself some little playtime. A few things: One, two male janitors work between five am and eleven am while the club is closed. One has a gun charge, and the other has drugs. I have their names and will run their socials and will run them back at the station in the morning. Two, there is a woman, Ms. Davendish, who has been causing trouble and a few fights with ladies and girls and has put a couple of girls in the hospital, which we will interview tomorrow after the janitors." He pointed to his right. She looked out the front window and saw two female deputies placing Ms. Davendish, who was nude and struggling, in a blanket and yelling for her Lawyer.

"If you feel it's a woman, why the janitors?" MacBride asked, fixing her shirt, realizing it was inside out. She also noticed that she no longer had her jacket.

"The one with the drug charge also has a medical degree, a surgeon from Brazil," Donovan answered, shifting, seeing someone he knew at the front of the club." And third, there's a woman in her sixties who has been working the room a lot over the last two months with girls that look like the girls in the morgue. I also have her name and social. You and I will follow her up with the janitors, and the hospital tomorrow. We'll be back, as a few staff and clients were not here tonight."

"Why not O'Malley and Stein?" MacBride asked, fixing her lipstick and putting the mirror back.

"O'Malley and Duke are going to find the Army vet who is holed up in the Sherman Forrest tomorrow."

"And Stein?"

"I think she and Alice will be recuperating more than you. I'll give her the day off and pick you up after I run the names and social in the morning," Donovan said, smiling and pointing at the entrance of the club with his left hand.

MacBride looked at him with an odd look, then glanced at the entrances, still others in line, as well as Rachel, and Robin, who had returned. She saw Alice out front dressed in a full leopard skin bodysuit, and two-inch heels, holding a riding crop in her left hand, and a leash in her right. The leash was connected to Stein's black leather and silver studded collar, wearing only two-inch black heels, a black leather bra, and panties, with a red ball gag in her mouth."

MacBride smiled, "About damn time Alice got some." both giggled.

"Yep, yep," Donovan said, driving off.

"If you knew I was into women, why didn't you out me with Marci the other day when I went off on her with her t-shirt that said 'I heart pussy'?"

"We were at the station. I played the asshole ex-husband against you so no one would realize or know that you visit the club or that you're into women. Because what happens at the Pearl Drop Club, stays at the Pearl Drop Club, until it comes out in my world or in the departments. I learned a long time ago, from Annabelle, that what happens with women is their business. Our Mom never knew about the club, and would have disowned her when she came out."

"And your dad?" Sarah asked quickly, remembering her seatbelt and quickly putting it on.

"We lost him when I was eight and Annabelle was eleven, on a case involving the Shermans," Donovan said as he pulled up to a two-story house with a large front yard and a long porch, dark red with white trim. A long driveway up the side with a covered parking stall.

"What if Marci or Gina came out?"

"If they're happy, then I am. I love them as much as I love you, as my best friend. But between each other, we have our own lives now."

"But now, I take it, I am your partner," MacBride said as they both stepped out of the car.

"Well, Stein will be busy with Roberts, and O'Malley will tromping the backwoods, so it's just us."

"Will you tell him?"

"Hell, I don't even know if this gig is long," Donovan said, walking her up to the door. A quick chirp sounded as he locked her car.

The Investigation

Donovan honked the horn of his classic sixty-six blue Mustang. Sarah wondered out slowly from the house, waking up, wearing the same outfit she had on the night before. Her shirt was tucked in the front and buttoned correctly with a different jacket, a bit darker than her blue slacks since her jacket was still at the club. She climbed in and said, "You said you were going to run the names and numbers, then we'll talk to the janitors. It's nine am, a bit early?"

He handed her a coffee and said, "You forget, a detective's job is twenty-four-seven. The captaincy must have made you soft," Donovan said.

MacBride looked straight at him harshly as she took the coffee and replied, "Yes."

"Remember, I said the guys were only there between five am and eleven am, and I have already run the names and socials."

She blocked the sun from her eyes with her hand.

Pulling up in front of the club, Donovan pounded on the door, no response. He pounded again, louder. Amanda opened the door, she is wearing a pink cotton robe, a black eye mask on her forehead, and pink slippers. "Why so early?"

"Your two janitors are only here till eleven, so two hours should give us enough time to talk and for you to find the last remaining staff and clients and get them here," Donovan explained.

Nodded, covering her eyes from the bright sun, they entered the main lobby. There were couches and benches along the walls, a long counter alone on their left side, and a concierge desk, like in a hotel. The lobby was large with black padded walls and six tall clear glass cases in the middle of the room, two double swinging doors opposite each other, labeled 'Ballroom' and 'Fetish Pit,' and a single large black wooden door near the long hallway to his far right, set into the wall, to Amanda's office.

MacBride looked at the cases and said, "Damn, I have only seen these at night, in dim light, with women all over and girls in different outfits in these cases – cheerleader, maid, nurse . . ." she commented as if neither Amanda nor Donovan had ever seen them. Donovan looked over at her from the corner of his eye, as if to stop her from rambling on and embarrassing herself more.

"Javier and Samuel are in the ballroom finish up," Amanda stated. Donovan handed her a list of names, and she quickly skimmed it. "The staff and all, but two of these I can have her within an hour. You do remember we open at three for clients, and we will need that time after twelve to set up."

"It will take as long as it will take, but as I said last night, we'll try not to disturb your clients," Donovan said and followed Amanda up to the ballroom doors.

Amanda opened the double doors to the ballroom, with the bar on their left. Javier was using a buffering machine on the dance floor, thirty, brown hair, and with a goatee. Samuel was off to their far left, wiping down tables, thirty also, and blonde. Amanda waved towards Javier to turn off the machine, which he did, then waved Samuel over. "These detectives wish to talk to you both," Amanda advised the two men.

Samuel walked over slowly, but Javier took off in a flash. "Why do they always run?" MacBride yelled.

"You got him?" Donovan called out. MacBride pulled her gun, aiming at Samuel, and Donovan followed, dropping his black notebook, which he was carrying, and darted out the back doors into the private rooms.

"Hands on your head, down on your knees," MacBride ordered, handing a set of cuffs to Amanda. "I know you know how to use these?"

Amanda smiled, taking the cuffs from her and cuffing his right hand atop his head, swinging it down, and cuffing his left hand.

Javier crashed through one of the rooms in the back, a gray stone façade of brick walls that covered the room, and with steel bars around a fake window. They crashed over a padded sawhorse in the middle of the room. Donovan followed him in, "Freeze!" Javier landed flat on his face and put his hands on his head. "On your knees!" Donovan said, pulling him up to cuff him. Then Donovan noticed the wall near the door with all sorts of bondage gear, whips, chains, and masks, and tossed him out the door.

Donovan returned him to the ballroom, put him on his knees near Samuel, and winded, walked over to Amanda, and he put his SIG back in his holster. "Sorry Amanda, he crashed into the dungeon room."

"How much damage?" Amanda asked, looking harshly down at Javier.

"Just the door and the horse are out of place."

She shook her head, fury rising, and knowing the amount it would cost to fix. "So now what?"

"You will need to hire two new janitors. Samuel here has a gun charge, and Javier here is a drug runner from Brazil and a Doctor," Donovan commented as he slammed his hand down onto Javier's shoulder. Amanda hauled off after them both, but Donovan stopped her.

"Call Duke and tell him to send backup and wait out front, please," Donovan advised MacBride.

Amanda pulled back from him. "You're both fired!"

"Does Duke know about this place?" MacBride asked, shifting toward the bar.

"Yes," Donovan said looking around.

The door to the club opened, and the two walked out slowly in cuffs. With MacBride behind them, two officers took each and put them into two separate cars. MacBride waited in the doorway as Duke met her. "This is not good for Belle."

"Yes…Are you and O'Malley heading out soon?" MacBride asked, hiding her eyes from the sunlight.

Duke nodded and returned to his patrol car. "Yes." turned to the other deputies. "Process them," then back at MacBride and drove off.

"The staff here, you asked for, they are in the ballroom. The two of the three clients you asked for are up in my office. Which first?"

Amanda asked, who was sitting back in the main lobby, taking notes. MacBride was leaning against the concierge desk.

Donovan and MacBride followed Amanda back into the ballroom as Amanda handed MacBride her coat back from the night before, the floor buffer still in the middle. Four servers, dressed for their shift, and three bartenders, still in street clothes, with Rachel at the end of the bar.

"First, I have some photos for you to look at and tell me if you know any of them and if you have seen them here before," Donovan said, taking photos out of his notebook.

"That's private, and you said …," Amanda said quickly, reminding him.

"All I need is a yes or no, nothing more," Donovan answered as he handed a photograph of the tattoo. First, each took it and looked it over, and then passed it down toward Rachel. Each shook their heads as if to say no. Amanda took the photograph from Rachel and looked it over herself. "Those are names we use here, but I prefer clean girls. None of my girls have tats."

Donovan collected the photograph and then handed out three photographs, each of the dead girls—family photographs, not crime scene shots. Rachel recognized two of the girls. "This one, here," she said, referring to the first girl they found in the forest, "I have seen her with Ms. Davendish a few times, and her, this one," she handed the photograph back to Donovan of the second girl, the one in white at the cemetery, "I have seen her with the old bitch, Ms. Stewart."

"The one I saw last night," Jacqueline said, "has been working the room hard these last two months?" Donovan asked, and Rachel nodded. "Any of the others?" The women looked at the photographs but shook their heads, no.

"Thank you very much, ladies," Donovan said, putting all the photographs back into his notebook.

Amanda looked at Rachel. "Get them back to work now!" as they all moved off quickly.

"I am sorry for the commotion. Sarah and I will be at the Hospital in a few hours, after talking to the clients upstairs. Can you meet us there?" Donovan asked with a sign of friendliness on his face.

"Yes, if this gets you out of my hair," Amanda said, walking out of the ballroom into the private back rooms.

"Might get me out of your hair, but I am still the owner," Donovan reminded her, as he giggled.

Up in her office, two older ladies waited. They were a bit embarrassed when Donovan and MacBride walked in. "It's ok, they just have a few questions about the girls you have seen on the news and in the papers, the ones in the forest and cemetery," Amanda explained, introducing them.

Donovan handed them a couple of his business cards. MacBride did the same. The older one of the two, a slightly graying blonde, quickly glanced at his card. "Ms. Annabelle?"

"My sister," Donovan said, leaning slightly on the back of the high-back chair across from them.

The first lady looked at the other, who was on the couch, and nodded to let her know it was okay. "How can we help you, Mr. Donovan?"

"I have a few photographs of the girls we found and wish to know if you knew them," Donovan explained, handing the first one the photographs.

"I don't wish to see dead bodies," the second lady with blue hair said.

"No, these are family photos," Donovan answered, handing them out. "All I need to know is if you recognize any of them and do you know their names, other than Plaything?"

They looked at him, then each other, and giggled, taking the photographs and looked them over. "Yes, I have seen them both and had a good time with this one a week ago," the first woman said, handing the photograph of the first girl back to Donovan.

"Do you remember when you two parted, was she okay? And where did she go after?" Donovan asked taking the photographs back.

"She and I were very okay," the gray-haired woman giggled. "I left and went to my car after dressing. She stayed in the room but she was alive, I know that much."

"One last question, I will be discreet. Did you use any bondage on her wrists or ankles?" Donovan asked, trying not to be too forward.

"No, she tied me down. I was her plaything that night," the blue-haired lady said with a bit of embarrassment and a big smile. "And she used me good." Both ladies giggled. She took the last photograph from the other lady and looked it over, pulling out the one with the red hair, one from the cemetery, who was in the white dress. "Yes, I danced with her a few nights and we cuddled in one of the booths, fingering. She just needed some love."

"How long ago was that?" MacBride asked. "Two weeks," she said.

"She was okay at the end of the night?" MacBride asked, leaning down more toward the woman.

"She was tired. I walked her to her car and I left in mine."

MacBride perked up, sitting next to the woman on the couch. "Do you remember the make and model, or license plate?"

"Not the plate. It was a white sports car, a convertible. I don't know the model."

"Thank you, ladies. You have been a big help," Donovan said, taking the photographs back and putting them in his notebook and toward Amanda slowly.

"Mr. Donovan," the First Lady stood and stepped near him, "We are truly sorry for your loss. Ms. Annabelle was an angel."

Donovan paused for a moment, thinking of his sister and knowing the love the club had for her, and then back at the woman and said, "Thank you."

In the main lobby, Sarah read the information on the back of the one identified girl's photograph, "Jennifer Michelson's parents forgot to tell us about her car."

"Yes, we need to talk to them again. We will stop at the station first and run her DMV record."

Donovan and MacBride walked up the path and rang the doorbell of the Michelsons' house. It was a single-story white house with a garage out front, and a path that winded back toward the front door. Mrs. Michelson answered the door, "Yes?" she was in her late forties with graying brunette hair.

Donovan raised his shield off his waist. "I am Lieutenant Donovan, and this is Captain MacBride. We have a few follow-up questions to finalize our case regarding your daughter. May we talk with you and your husband briefly?"

"Any answers on my baby's death?" Mrs. Michelson asked, still behind the screen door.

"Not yet, but I think with a few follow-up questions, we feel it will help us move forward in identifying the suspect," Donovan explained.

Mr. Michelson opened the door more. "Whose is it, Martha?" he asked, with dark brown hair, in his fifties, with some graying around his temples, and wearing black-framed glasses.

"More police, Stanley!" She answered him, trying to hold her tears back. "We have done all the talking we are going to do! Please, no more."

"I only wanted to know where her car was. A witness saw her leave work in it, that night of her disappearance. The DMV has no record of her owning a vehicle." Donovan explained.

Mrs. Michelson ran back into the house while Mr. Michelson stepped outside, closing the door. He was wearing a white sweater and blue jeans pointing with his hand for them to move back from the door. They moved down the path and around to the front of the garage. "I've always known where my daughter worked . . . at that damn Lesbian club. But Martha doesn't know. She thinks she is a server at the IHOP in the next town over. And I would like to leave it that way, please?" Donovan nodded. MacBride rolled her eyes at the way he said 'Lesbian club,' as he continued, "She had one of my cars that night. I own a dealership in North Mammoth, and she has been using it for the last three months while working there." He pulled a card from his wallet. "I do not know where the car is now, and I reported it stolen a week ago. Here is my insurance card for that car. This might help you. It has the VIN and license plate. I hope this helps." MacBride took the card, and they walked back toward the Mustang.

"That bastard! It's not a damn lesbian club or brothel. It is a place for women to be alone with other women and explore their sexual desires and fantasies away from men!" MacBride yelled. "Over 80 percent are not lesbians as he said," She paused, watching his reaction.

"What?" he asked, with a smile.

"You agree with him!"

"No, I do not agree with him. And if I did, would I have helped Annabelle? As I told you before, a woman's business is her own. I love and respect her and you. If I agree with anyone, I agree with you. But I do love it when you get angry," he answered and drove off. MacBride smiled.

Donovan and MacBride walked up the path to the hospital and saw Amanda in a black tight business suit, outside, very tight to the skin, and putting a cigarette out. Only her hands and ankles were visible, with two-inch heels. Men looked her over, some wives and girlfriends slapped them for looking at her, and there were a few nurses and women around the entrance also checking her out and whispering. The whole town believed she was the local Madam.

"Two of the three are still here. The other was discharged earlier today, and she will be at my office in two days if that is alright with you?" Amanda said, looking at Donovan, and she was not pleased to be there.

"That will be fine. Lead the way," Donovan answered. Amanda led them inside, down the hall past the admission desk, and around a corner to their right, and waited for the elevator. Amanda pushed the fifth floor button and said, "Abigail Johnson, one of the girls, at the ballroom is here. She has a broken arm and has been beaten up pretty bad. Margo Kingston, same floor, has a virginal tearing and has been beaten."

"Do you know if either of them has any anal damage?" Donovan asked.

Amanda looked at him sharply with shock and replied, "Not that I am aware of."

The floor rang, the doors opened, and they stepped off, seeing an older nurse waiting with a teen boy in a wheelchair. His eyes widened at the sight of Amanda. They walked to their right, down a hallway up toward a nurse's desk. Donovan waved MacBride ahead. She walks up to the desk, and showed her shield, saying, "We need to talk with Abigail Johnson and Margo Kingston privately."

The nurse looked the rooms up on the computer, "Yes, five-fifteen and five-twenty-one," she answered and pointed to her right.

"This way," MacBride said, showing them the way.

Amanda knocked gently, opening the door a bit, "Margo, are you awake?"

"Yes," a low scared female voice answered.

Margo Kingston, blonde in her early twenties, was lying on her back in bed, with a few bandages on her swollen face, "How are you doing, Margo?" Margo quickly saw Donovan and was not happy, and pulled back, "It's ok, this is Donovan, Ms. Annabelle's brother. Its ok, you can trust him."

She relaxed some, and with a hoarse voice, and swollen, she said, "You're T.K?"

"Yes, I just have a couple of questions, and then we'll leave you alone," Donovan said. She looked at Amanda again and then back at Donovan, and nodded, "I will be discreet and quick. First, who did this to you?"

"I told you, who did this, Donovan," Amanda yelled and ran up to Donovan, but MacBride pulled her back.

MacBride leaned over to Amanda and whispered, "He needs to legally ask, otherwise it could be taken as hearsay, and not admissible in court."

"Margo, take your time," Donovan said.

She looked down at the bed, and then back up at the wall, and Amanda stepped followed some, and whispered, "It's okay, he knows everything. He has been the silent partner since Ms. Annabelle's death. He won't use your name."

"Ms. Davendish," Margo said, slowly trying to hold the pain and tears back.

"This one may be a hard one, but I need to know . . . how?" Donovan asked but wished he did not have to.

She started to cry, closed her eyes, "She used a plunger handle, several times inside me, and beat me with it," and then she looked back, away from him and at the wall, not letting him see her tears.

"Where?" Donovan asked softly.

Staring at the wall, she let out a heavy sigh, and then turned back toward him, ". . . the basement."

Amanda's face turned beet red, "Fuck, no! She is not allowed down there."

Margo looked over at Amanda, "she grabbed me by my hair outside the ballroom, dragged me down to the basement, calling me a whore and a piece of shit." she said quickly and very scared.

Donovan placed his hand down on her hand, "Thank you, you have done well, I am done, and I am sorry," he walked out followed by MacBride. He sat down on a bench in the hallway, writing his notes from all she had told him.

He finished as Amanda came out, "So you have enough to arrest her?"

"Enough to bring her back in for questioning, but let's talk with Abigail," Donovan said, standing and walking down the hall.

Amanda stiffened up and composed herself, walked down the hallway, knocked on the second door, and opened it some, "Abigail, can we come in?"

"Yes?" She was lying with her left arm in a sling, blonde hair, mid-twenties, seeing Donovan and started shaking, but Amanda walked up quickly and whispered, "He is Ms. Annabelle's brother. He's okay. Just answer his question, please." She nodded.

"All I need to know is how, where, and what was done, please? Take your time."

Abigail, still crying, looked from Donovan over to Amanda. "Ms. Davendish... one of the dungeon rooms, she broke my arm because I kept calling out my safe word, but she wouldn't stop."

"I am sorry, I just have one last question, OK? Did she rape you?" Donovan asked patiently, already knowing the answer.

Her tears increased, she looked at Amanda with fear in her eyes, and Amanda nodded.

"Both holes?" Donovan asked, not looking at her. He could not feel her pain, but something hurt inside him, too.

Trying to hold her tears back, she replied, "Both."

He placed his hand on her hand. "Thank you." He turned and walked out. MacBride followed, he wrote his notes again, but this time leaning against the wall.

"Why didn't you ask Margo about rape?" MacBride asked.

"She had vaginal tearing, so we can conclude there was a rape," Donovan answered her without looking up from his notebook.

"Well?" Amanda yelled.

"Yes, I will have Stein and Scott pick her up, once I get the warrants."

Suspects

Donovan sat at a long table in the bullpen where the whiteboard was. Stein was at her desk, working on paperwork. Sarah walked in from interrogation, and walked down the hallway past her office into the bullpen. O'Malley was not present, and other officers were working at their desks or moving around, continuing their daily assignments. Maria was at the check-in desk. Donovan spotted from the corner of his eye, three men enter, all in dress blues; two are in their late forties to early fifties, each with two stars on their epaulets. One was Asian, and the other was White, each carrying a file box. The third man was in his late sixties, with gray hair, and four stars on his epaulets, with silver frame glasses. They stopped just inside, past the check-in desk.

"Attention!" MacBride called out, and all stopped and came to attention. Donovan turned a bit toward them. The three men walked up to MacBride and saluted.

"You're not in uniform, Missy," the sheriff said. He turned and walked over to Donovan, while his two aides waited. "Your Father never gave me the respect either, son, but you will," the old Sheriff said, kicking the stool out from under him. He dropped to the floor but got back up quickly, with a fist drawn. Duke stepped up from behind, who was also working at the table, and held him back. "Your Father was a good man, a respected cop, and he never walked away from a job."

"Sir, he didn't walk away. I suspended him, per the city council," MacBride said from across the room.

The Sheriff turned toward her briefly, then back to Donovan. "Your office, Mister. Now!" He ordered, walking toward Donovan's office. Donovan regained his composure and looked right at Duke, and continued to his office. MacBride turned and waved the others to return to their duties.

The old Sheriff sat behind Donovan's desk. "Close the door," Donovan did, but was not happy that this man was using his office. "We need to talk."

"Why would you disrespect my father, your best friend, in front of his brother-in-law, Duke, and the men and women of this department? His department?" Donovan said, slamming the desk.

The Sheriff looked at him sternly. "My Department, Son, but you need to tread softly on the Sherman business," he said, staring at him. Donovan half looked at him, did the Sheriff know he had gone up to the old woman's estate. "Your father was a good cop and tried to find out what was going on up there also, and it cost him his life. I don't wish that to happen to you."

Donovan looked back at Duke through the large glass window of his office, seeing Duke looking back at him, and watched him leave, quickly. "Duke and your reports stated it was an accident from a DUI case?" Donovan asked, sitting down on the couch.

The Sheriff stood, snapped his fingers, and pointed at the door. His two aides entered, placed the boxes on Donovan's desk, and quickly left. "These may help you," the Sheriff said as he started to leave, and stopped, then leaned down and whispered, "That old bitch may not be your killer, but she is connected. Take her down, honor your Father, and finish his last case. Be a good son and soldier," The Sheriff advised him. Donovan sat up and half-leaned, looking out the doorway, watching the old Sheriff and his aides leave. He knew right then that something was not adding up. There was a lot to this he did not remember growing up, or from the two files he found in evidence, and he was still not sure why Duke ran out as he did.

MacBride and Stein joined him. MacBride turned the boxes around. The label read: 'Lieutenant Malachi A. Donovan.'

Donovan looked up. "Have you sent any reports up the line or informed anyone of *our* trip up to the Sherman Estate?" Donovan asked, crossing back behind his desk and looking over the top box.

"No, we've all been following leads and bodies," MacBride answered.

Donovan opened the lid on the top box and ran his finger over the files inside. "I have some more light reading to do," he said and turned back toward the bullpen, scanning it closely for Duke. MacBride looked out and knew he was looking for Duke. After all that had just transpired, he had more questions for his old Uncle.

Roberts strolled into the bullpen, wearing a black business suit with a skirt, pulling an oversized carryall bag and a small black single-strap purse. She had a bit more makeup than normal and with a look of more confidence, unlike she has had in the past. She entered Donovan's office, all noticing her, especially Stein with her eyes slightly down. Roberts gave a quick unnoticeable nod back. Donovan noticed it as she placed her purse on the couch, resting her oversized bag against it, pulled out a few files, and handed them to Donovan. "Final reports on the first ten victims," Roberts advised as she offered them to him. Stein moved a bit closer.

"Shall we take this to the conference room?" Donovan said, looking from Roberts to Stein. Stein followed Roberts out and pulled her carryall bag, as Roberts took the folders back.

MacBride stepped closer to Donovan. "Did you see how Dana responded to Alice?"

Donovan skimmed one of the files from his Father's boxes. "What happens at the Pearl Drop. . ."

"Stays at the Pearl Drop, I know, I know," MacBride said, mocking him under her breath leaving his office and continued onto the conference room. Donovan still scanning the bullpen for Duke and started for the conference room, but first opened the center drawer and placed the two folders of evidence from his father's case. He found them in the evidence room, placed them into the boxes, and closed them. "Hanson!"

Hanson stepped into his office. "Yes, sir?"

"Take these to my car, please," he asked, handing him his keys. Hanson left, and Donovan moved toward the conference room.

"Donovan ol' man! Good to see you again," McKnight called out from the check-in desk with an oversized wheeled carryall bag himself, in a very nice tailored ruby red suit. "Looks like I made it just in time.

Alice called and said she was going to give her reports. Thought I would bring the Forensic reports."

"The more the merrier, Mac," Donovan said, as he put his hand out toward the conference room. "Maria? When you see Duke again, please have him wait for me." She nodded, and he entered the conference room.

Roberts took the far end of the table, Stein to her left with the wall to her back, and helped her with the files, placing out copies, as McKnight and MacBride took their chairs on the window wall. Donovan closed the door and sat at the end closest to the door and opened the top folder of the stack that Stein placed in front of him.

"All female victims, ranging from sixteen to twenty-five spanning nine weeks, each as we saw dressed in elegant black or white ball gowns. Each having teardrop Pearl Necklaces, and each having been tied by the ankles and wrists. They had been held for at least five to seven days, suffering from severe dehydration, sexual intercourse, and rape, both pre-and post-mortem in both orifices," Roberts explained with the folder open, standing and placing photographs of the bruising on each wrist or ankle on the whiteboard, on the wall behind her.

Each looked over the folders they had. McKnight skimmed a page and asked, "Did any of the other girls have blunt force trauma? We had discussed this the other day with Dr. Bayer at the University."

"No, only the first girl had a sharp indentation along the back of her head, along her Occipital Lobe, and the back of her neck," Roberts said as she touched the back of her neck, "from a fall or being slammed into something. All the others were suffocated by hand strangulation. I found very faint finger impressions around their necks," she pointed at a photograph of the first girl's neck on the wall with very thin, faint red handprints, as Stein took her hands around Roberts' neck, thumbs overlapping below her chin as if they had done so many times before in private play. "The suspect strangled the girls this way, well on top of them, as a conclusion with the missionary position during sex. The force of the hands matches the force of brushing on the inner thighs as a downward force during sex," she explained as Stein sat back down, and Roberts pointed back at the photograph.

McKnight handed out files with his left hand, also a southpaw like Donovan, from his carryall. "Forensics went over all the dresses, necklaces, and found very little trace evidence," Alice found from her examination of the bodies, "and my team found that the dresses and the girls were clean, most likely bathed before being dressed again. Each had panties, but we found no bras. We found no trace evidence in the panties, except for the cards Alice found when she disrobed them before the autopsies. The dresses were from a mail-order company out of Taiwan, as well as the panties. We found no credit card or payment receipt for these items for the last two years. Either our suspect had them already or stolen them from another party."

Both Donovan and MacBride knew where the gowns and necklaces came from. Amanda had bulk ordered them for the Pearl Drop Club. As well as knowing Stein and Roberts were aware now, after seeing them at the club, Donovan now knew the connection and remembered where he had seen the girls before.

"What about the yellow flakes I found at the scene with the most recent girls in Sherman's forest?" Stein asked.

"From what we could tell," McKnight said as he skimmed a page in a folder, "metal paint flakes. Each girl had them in small amounts in wrist wounds, which, as we all know, were cut off. Most likely an old hacksaw with a yellow blade," he said, as he placed a newly purchased one on the table in a bag for comparison.

"So either the suspect is very good or knows how to clean a scene up very well," Donovan said.

Hanson entered the room quickly. "Sorry, Captain, but you'll need to see this!" He turned the television on, which was sitting on a cart in the corner opposite the door. The screen showed the blonde-haired reporter O'Malley pushed back at Sherman's forest, outside the sheriff's station. In a live telecast, *"As we reported earlier today, People and contacts I have spoken with are calling him, the Pearl Drop Killer, there have been seventeen female bodies, between the ages of sixteen and thirty, discovered in Sherman's forest and the Sherman cemetery. Each was dressed in a White or Black ball-type gown and wearing a teardrop Pearl necklace. We have had no comments from the Sheriff's Department, Captain MacBride, or Lieutenant Donovan. As he has been in the past, tight-lipped. Lieutenant Donovan is keeping us out of the loop. Detective O'Malley declined a statement when the first bodies were discovered in Sherman's forest."* The video cuts to the Sherman's forest showing O'Malley instructing the deputies to move back the reports. *"Ten, no, twenty feet, or more!" So again, this community is in the dark about who has and is killing our young girls. . ."*

"Off!" MacBride yelled as she slammed her fist down on the table. Hanson shut off the television, turned to leave, and saw O'Malley and Duke walking a very shaggy and dirty man with brown hair, with some grey, and a long shaggy beard, looking as if he had not showered or cleaned in months. The man was dressed in solid green fatigues and a jacket, and black combat boots.

"Great! O'Malley caught the Unabomber," Stein said.

The man was fighting both men, kicking and pushing, knocking papers and items off nearby desks, and knocking Duke to the floor, as others grabbed him and tried to help restrain him. They watched as Duke, O'Malley, and now Hanson, who had run out to join them, along with other deputies to control the hermit, and walked him down past MacBride's office to the interrogation room.

Donovan and MacBride turned back to the table. "This is going to be good," Donovan said.

"Think he did it?" Stein asked.

"No, but he may be involved, but I believe with all that we have seen and from what Alice has found through her autopsies, and how they were raped with a strap-on, like the one Alice showed us," McKnight looked at Roberts swung his upper body slightly, as if to say, 'You go girl.' "We may have a female serial killer. I will talk with him first and then give my profile out," Donovan explained.

Captain Grant sat behind the table in the interrogation room across from Donovan and O'Malley. He had a stern cold look without moving his hands, which were in cuffs, and attached to a ring on the table. "He gave us a run for our money, and Ranger Rick was right. He Rambo'd us too. We lost him for a time, but then found him. Found him way up in Sherman's forest, in a cave, which was well stocked."

"You never read me my rights," Grant said in a low voice.

"You're not under arrest. We just have some questions, and we were told you were in the area during the time of the body dump by

Ranger Rick and others," Donovan said, opening two files he had with him.

Grant jerked fast and pulled his cuffs tight, looking at Donovan as if to ask why the cuffs were necessary. "You gave me and my men a hard time, broke two of their noses and twisted one man's arm nearly off. There for your safety and ours," O'Malley said.

"Your files state," Donovan said, reading his complete record, which Stein got from her army friend, "Three tours in the Gulf, Army surgeon, dishonorably discharged for the rape and torture of four army nurses. Served ten years in Leavenworth and released four years ago."

"He didn't serve long enough," O'Malley said. Grant turned his head slowly toward him.

"Then came here and have been living up in the mountains. What brought you here?" Donovan said as he leaned forward slightly.

"My late wife's family lives here, my only family," Grant replied, looking straight at Donovan.

Donovan looked over his record again. "It does not state here that you're married."

"Common law, before I signed up."

"What family would have you?" O'Malley said with disgust.

Grant looked around the room slowly, gazing up at the mirror behind them, knowing he was being watched. Then slowly looked at O'Malley, then back at Donovan. "Sherman."

There it was again, that name. It kept flashing at Donovan like a blinding red light. "Sorry for your loss, but when and how did your wife die?" Donovan asked coldly.

Grant looked down then back at up Donovan, knowing this was a joke. They had nothing. "Cancer. I was still in Kansas when I got word from her Sister."

"So, since your return, you have lived up in the mountains, above the forest," Donovan asked, looking through the second folder.

"Yeah, Old Lady Sherman does not like the fact that her daughter and I were shaking up and had a rule: no men in the house, period, since old man Sherman passed. I knew about the caves from when I was a kid and went there," Grant explained, shifting in his chair.

"And living off the land this whole time?" Donovan asked.

"You needed others? All the shit I saw in your cave, you needed help hiking it back up there," O'Malley added.

"Broderick's Trading Post twice a month, I go down, get supplies, shoot the breeze, and hear the news from old man Broderick and his sons," Grant said, scratching his beard.

"So, the ranger saw you there?" Donovan asked, looking over the report from O'Malley, which the Ranger gave him.

"Yeah, I was returning from there. Old man Broderick needed a fifth player for his poker game the night before."

O'Malley wrote something in his small notebook and handed it to Donovan, and he quickly read it. "And that night, he chased you near the cliff?"

Grant looked cross-eyed at O'Malley. "No, I saw him at his pot farm on my way to the cave, and he came at me. I ran."

"Did you see anyone else that you normally did not see that day between the time you left Broderick's and found the Ranger's pot farm?" Donovan asked, putting the paper in one of the folders.

Grant closed his eyes slowly, paused, thinking, and then opened them, blowing out gently. "Other than hunters coming in that day for the season, there was a woman who asked for directions."

"What woman?" O'Malley asked, cutting Donovan off before his next question.

"Late twenties, maybe early thirties, big lady, white, long brunette hair, and looked like she lifted weights and worked out a lot. Black jeans, gray sweatshirt, sleeves cut off, long slit down the side, no bra, and damn big tits."

"Stay on topic," Donovan said.

"She was asking for directions to the cemetery."

"What type of vehicle was she driving?" O'Malley asked quickly.

"An old beat-up van, side windows darkened, and a broken window in the back, no tire on the hitch."

"What color and how do you know that?" O'Malley asked pushing for more, and stood up, irritated but not scaring Grant, who just sat there with a small smile.

"After she left, I stepped outside to pee, and she asked for help. She was looking inside the engine. Tan in color, Ford 'Econoline' Cargo, few years old, maybe fifteen years, its emblem was on the engine panel."

"How did you know the window was broken and the hitch had no tire?" O'Malley asked slamming the table.

Donovan pulled him back, and they whispered. He told him to take it easy, then looked back at Grant. "She called from the front. I was peeing at the rear of the van, near the steps in front of the trading post, and the van windows were either frosted or blackened. I jiggled a wire near the sparkplugs and told her to try it again, and it started. She asked me again for directions, and then left."

"How do you know this, in all that details?" Donovan asked, looking closely at him.

"As a surgeon, especially the fine detail work I do on hands and wrist, I need to be detail-oriented," Grant said, picking and biting his fingernails.

"Anything else, you remember?" Donovan asked closing the folders.

"Went back inside, shot the breeze with a few of the hunters, then Dan Broderick, the oldest son asked me to join them on a hunt, which he had planned for early that morning. I declined."

Donovan leaned over and whispered to O'Malley, and then turned back to Grant, "We are going to hold you until we check out your story, okay?"

"Whatever," Grant said, with his eyes glaring harshly toward O'Malley.

MacBride, Stein, and McKnight were standing outside the room, after coming from the adjacent room, watching it all through the one-way mirror on the other side. "Then he is our suspect?" Stein asked.

"I don't know. As I said, the killer is female, but I do think he is involved, he has too much information for a casual fix of the van and has the skills to cut each wrist off. Mac, call your team. I want you to go over him with a fine-tooth comb. Then let him clean himself up and put him in a new cell. Then check that cell. Continue watching him, one deputy outside his cell and another in the cell next to him, on a suicide watch," Donovan explained, looking from McKnight to Stein, and finally to O'Malley.

Donovan walked off toward the bullpen, MacBride followed him, and McKnight continued back into the conference room. "Duke is in your office," MacBride said.

"Thank you, and can you find out who leaked the story to Camille and the other reporters, please?" MacBride nodded, and he continued into his office.

Donovan slammed the door hard, the sound resonating through the bullpen. "Thought we were family, Duke!"

"I know, T. It was Malachi's dying wish that you would not know the true circumstances surrounding his death," Duke said with heavy remorse on his face and in his voice.

"You could have at least told me two days ago when I commented on the Sherman link to this case," Donovan said as he sat down behind his desk.

"I know, but the Sheriff told me not to say a word, till he talked to you. I am truly sorry, Bratanek," Duke said, calling him nephew in Polish.

"Stop calling me Nephew. I love you and respect you, but you hurt me," he stood and placed his hand on the boxes the Sheriff gave him. "Tell me what's not in here?" Donovan said, tapping one of the boxes with his thumb.

Duke sat back. "It was never reported, but I believed the bullets from the shotgun that killed your Dad were gravel and bacon greases, not standard buckshot shells. The Sheriff, who was Captain at the time, told me to report it as shells. We know that Old Lady Sherman still had her late husband's shotgun, and he used bacon grease and gravel many times to kill rodents and shoot at trespassers."

"What about the Sherman house? I know Dad would have got a warrant and searched it completely."

"Most of the reports are in there, except. . . The Sheriff changed the reports. We had found evidence that there had been young girls, between eight and fourteen, in the house, in a few rooms, and down in the basement, in chains, with only food and water bowls for eating and drinking, like dogs or cats."

"No bodies, just evidence?" Donovan asked sitting on the desk and pushing the boxes over some.

"Yes, it was a different back then," Duke squirmed some, looking around, "The Sheriff didn't want it to get out that the old lady had a thing for little girls, both sexually and abusively."

Donovan leaned back, listening and remembering what Jock told him of the rumors, "Yea, twenty-five years ago, no one accepted that homosexuality happened in this town, too sinful at the time for this community."

"Yes, still very backward today," Duke said.

"Please detail all the facts you remember of my Father's death and the case, which were omitted, leave nothing out," Donavan said standing up and offering Duke his hand.

Duke nodded, Stein knocked on the door, and he waved her in. "Mayor Whitefield telephoned and asked if you and the Captain would meet her for tea up at her house."

"Did you inform the Captain?" Donovan asked and Duke stood up to leave. Stein nodded.

"Be careful, T," Duke advised him.

MacBride and Donovan sat in a garden across a glass table with Mayor Whitefield, who was in a flowery sundress, no bra, and pouring tea from a ceramic teapot into a few cups. "Sugar or honey?" She asked as she looked and poured more for him.

"None for me, please," Donovan said.

"Honey, please," MacBride asked.

"So, why have you invited us for tea, Mayor?" Donovan asked.

Mayor Whitefield sipped her tea. "I wanted to personally apologize for the news report and ask how your investigation is going." Donovan shot a stern look at MacBride. "Donovan, is there anything my office can do to assist you in your investigation?" Donovan could tell she was fishing.

"At this time, it's an ongoing investigation. We are following up on leads, questioning witnesses, and following all the evidence that forensics and the ME find, wherever it leads," Donovan said looking straight at her.

Whitefield sipped more, and looked around. "And how is the club involved?"

"No need to worry, Ma'am. A few leads lead us to the club, but nothing that concerns yourself, or the town learning of yours and any of the women's extracurricular activities there," Donovan replied.

Whitefield smiled over at MacBride. "Good, good, but if there is anything I can do to help, just ask."

Donovan shifted in his chair. getting irritated. MacBride spoke. "Miss, You can trust us. All that is being done is being done, and I don't think you wish to be named in association with us or when we may have to mention where the evidence leads us."

"Oh, yes, yes. I do see your point, Captain. I am sorry I wasted your time," Whitefield said, and they stood. "She will show you out," as she waved at a maid, who was standing near the house, an African American woman in her late fifties, in a black dress with a white apron.

Returning to the car, MacBride leaned over toward Donovan, "Do you think she is getting worried?"

"Not about the case, but about her extracurricular activities," Donovan replied as he waved back at Whitefield, who was at the front door now, waving at them.

"You ready to give the Profile?"

"After we stop by Mac's office and get the preliminary report, his team should be done with Captain Grant by now," Donovan said as he climbed into the passenger side.

Both sat in McKnight's office across his desk in the forensics lab, in a spacious office that sits among many offices, labs, and a couple of interrogation rooms, all surrounded by glass walls. Behind his desk is a long bookshelf with books and jars of specimens he had collected over the years. McKnight entered with a couple of folders and sat behind his desk. "We found engine grease on the cuffs of his sleeves, and blood and urine from many animals on both his pant legs and jacket sleeves."

"Human blood and or tissues?" Donovan asked.

"Yes, his own, mostly on his pants, but no other human trace, and a lot of animals, mainly deer, bear, and possum."

"Makeup or gold flakes?" MacBride asked.

"No, but we did find chalk on his hands and pant legs."

"Chalk, like weightlifters would use?" Donovan asked, taking a folder from McKnight.

"Possibly, but it's only a preliminary report."

"When I was at the club the first night, Ms. Amanda asked a young woman, who was large for her size and could have been a weightlifter, her name was Jacqueline, to show me around. I saw chalk on her hands," Donovan commented.

"Don't know her at the club," MacBride stated, Mac's eyes widened.

"Might be time to return and talk to her?" Donovan said.

Donovan, now driving in front of the club, saw Rachel watching them. Donovan pointed to the back, and Rachel looked to Robin, who entered the club. Amanda opened the backdoor, wearing a black leather spandex bodysuit. "This better be good, Donovan, I was having fun!"

"I am not entering. I am looking for the woman. Jacqueline, you told me to show me around the other day. Get her, please?" Donovan ordered.

"She has not been to work since you were here two nights ago," Amanda said.

Donovan looked at MacBride. "If she does show up, please call me, but don't let her know I came," Amanda just let the door go, and it slammed shut in front of him.

"Now what?" MacBride asked.

"She may have thought I was onto her after that night, after our talk up in Amanda's office about the girls, and with what the news reported. We'll put out an APB and BOLO on her and her van, and I want to talk with Grant some more," Donovan said.

"Time for the profile?" MacBride asked, not knowing what to do next.

"Let's find her first. Call Dana, and have her call the club officially and get her employee file."

Donovan walked into the cells below the bullpen. "You were in the van!"

Grant looked up at him. "Yes, I told you, I worked on the engine."

"No, you were in the van. We found weightlifter's chalk on your hands and pants, you and she probably wrestle in the back. A quickie?" Donovan said, stepping up to the bars.

"Fuck no, she's a fucking dyke! That Nigger bitch next to you is more her type!" Grant yelled and looked coldly at Stein, who was standing next to him. "There was chalk all over the stinking van. She drove, and I gave directions to the cemetery."

"How did you know she's into women, and did you look in the back?

"There were girly mags all over the place, teen girly mags from Europe, and I could see she had a package in her pants the whole time. She was strapped, and it was thick, check with the Trading Post, they all saw it. The back was empty and dark, no bodies, if that is what you are asking." Grant answered, looking straight at him.

"How do you know I meant bodies?" Donovan asked.

"She was going to the cemetery. I heard from Dan, the news had reported on the missing girls, and then I read in the papers, the three found in the cemetery," Grant said still not looking or standing up.

Moving closer to the bars, "Why didn't you tell me this in the first place?"

Grant turned fast and stood. "You think I am that stupid? If I told you, you would have thought it was me who killed those girls or even helped her."

"Did you?" Stein asked.

"No, I directed her to the cemetery, and she left me there. I hiked back to my cave. I could tell when I was walking away that she was at the Sherman's tombstone for a long time."

"Did you know her before that day?" Donovan asked.

Shifting closer, "Nope, never seen her, before."

Donovan turned, and a guard unlocked the door to the stairs. "May I go now?" Grant yelled, but Donovan and Stein walked out, and the guard closed and locked the door.

"May I go now?" Grant yelled louder from the cell, standing and pushing on the bars.

MacBride waited at the top of the stairs, and handed him a pink file with a martini glass and kitten on the cover. "Ms. Amanda stated she hopes you're officially done with the Club?"

"Hardly," Donovan said, opening the file. "Duke, O'Malley!" he yelled out, handing the file to Stein and running toward the bullpen.

Stein opened the folder, and looked up at MacBride, who was nodding. "Jacqueline Sherman!"

Playthings

The white Mercedes-Benz SLS convertible rose slowly from the lake, dragged by the towline of a tow truck winch. McKnight and Hanson stood off to the side, leaning against Hanson's squad car, water rushing out the wheel wells and from small openings where the doors touched the frame and the engine. The white convertible now covered in muddy lake water rolled slowly up the embankment, Hanson took the insurance card Michelson's Father gave MacBride from his shirt pocket and compared the VIN.

"Does it match?" McKnight asked.

Hanson gave a thumbs up as the truck driver dropped the Convertible with a loud thud and rocked the shocks back and forth. Both men look over the car, Hanson on the driver's side, McKnight on the passenger. *Nothing out of the ordinary, but the water could have washed it away*, McKnight thought, as he continued to the rear. "Pop it," McKnight ordered.

Hanson grabbed a crowbar from another deputy and popped the lock at the base of the trunk. The trunk lifted with some water cascading out and dripping, both look inside, blue nylon ropes, cut into short lengths and four red and white ball gags.

They looked at each other. "Alice stated the victims were tied down with rope. These do match the fibers my team found along the wrist and ankles, and these must have been used to keep them quiet," McKnight explained, as he picked up one of the balls gags with his ballpoint pen through the clasp. Then motioned to two male forensic techs that were standing off behind the tow truck. "Bag these and get them to the lab. Better informed Donovan we found it." McKnight stated. Hanson nodded as the forensic techs moved into work.

"Listen up everyone," Donovan called out in the bullpen, "Our suspect is, Jacqueline Sherman."

"Female?" Maria asked.

"Yes, in rare cases, less than nine percent are females, and less than two percent of them, are same-sex perpetrators. I want an APB and a BOLO out, Captain MacBride will give you all the details. She may be armed and dangerous, so be careful. If anyone spots her, contact me or O'Malley, do not engage alone," Stein and MacBride stepped up and joined him, "I need Ms. Davendish picked up and brought in for questioning. Stein has her home address and hospital contacts. Ms. Davendish is not associated with Ms. Sherman but is needed for questioning in a different case," Donovan explained and waved them off.

Jock ran in, wearing blue jeans and a grey sweatshirt, and up to Donovan and MacBride, "Did either of you two pick up the girls today?"

Both looked at each other, "No."

"Then they're missing, I went to the school to pick them up, and they were not there, the school told me, you," he said, as he pointed at Donovan, "had called them in sick."

"Their missing!" MacBride yelled.

"I checked the school, your house, and your trailer at the Bar, T, and then came here," Jock explained, looking from MacBride to then Donovan.

"Donovan, *my* girl?" MacBride yelled with a loud sigh.

"Will find 'em," Donovan said.

"She has them."

"We don't know that. Marci may just be pissed off from the argument you and she had the other day and ran off," Donovan said holding Sarah close.

Duke handed him a piece of paper. "Got another body, T."

"A sixteen-year-old, near the park, and the girl's school," Donovan read the paper out loud.

"Donovan!" She grabbed him and dropped to her knees crying.

"Amber Alert, Duke," Donovan ordered.

O'Malley's SUV came to a squelching stop, with lights flashing. O'Malley, Duke, and Donovan climbed out fast, racing past the tapeline, as Scott raised it. A sixteen-year-old girl, with blonde hair, a teardrop pearl necklace, and a set of white gloves, a white ball gown laid on the ground, but this time, she was in her belly, not her back as the others, her face had been badly beaten and still bloody. Tossed from a moving vehicle, unlike the others, not laid down under the underbrush and covered with care, very sloppy, Donovan thought.

Donovan and O'Malley lean down over the body as they hear another car come to a squelching halt and they look up. Donovan ran back to the tapeline grabbing MacBride, "Marci!" MacBride yelled.

"It's not her, Sarah, it's not her," Donovan said, holding her as she was crying on his shoulder.

She stepped back, "I want to see her?"

He nodded, "But you're not staying," leading her up toward the body, Scott raised the tapeline again, reaching the body, she turned away, holding Donovan tight, "Duke, take her back to the car, please?"

Duke took her from Donovan as Stein joined them, "This looks sloppy and quick, sure it's the same person?" Stein asked.

"Yes, she's devolving and might know we're on to her," Donovan replied.

O'Malley pressed on the girl's arm, "No rigor, she's fresh."

"Has the area been searched?" Donovan asked.

Hanson and Scott walked up, "Yes, still looking over the park, the school is in lockdown and still searching room by room, evacuating the students and staff as we go. We have found a backpack, and a box in the library, the bomb squad is en route." Scott reported, "We also found Michelson's car in Sherman's lake, this morning," Hanson reported, Donovan nodded.

Roberts joins them, he waves her team in,

"T!" O'Malley pointed to a piece of notebook paper under the girl's left shoulder."

"Leave the paper till the body is moved?" Donovan said looking at Roberts, "Let's go, O'Malley," they headed off toward the school.

Donovan and O'Malley walked past the tapeline outside the high school library, which sat in the center of the campus, Camille and her camera crews were near the tapeline with other reports, "Care to comment now, Detective Donovan?"

"No Comment!" Donovan yelled and continued.

"The new body at the park, is it associated with the current serial killer or something new?" Camille yelled.

O'Malley turned back as Donovan walked on, "He said, No comment, Bitch!" Camille cowered a bit and O'Malley continued toward the library.

A bomb squad technician slowly exited the library in full gear, padding over his legs and body, with 'SWAT' on the chest pad, with large side padding around his head and neck, with an oversized helmet and glass shield. "All clear L.T.," the older African American man said taking his helmet off, he was in his late fifties. "We checked the pack and box, no explosives."

Donovan nodded as the man walked off. Donovan opened the door as O'Malley caught up to him, each putting on fresh gloves.

Sitting on a single table in the center of the room, the other tables moved away from the center, clearing a blast path if there was a bomb. A medium-sized cardboard box sat on the table, cut open. A black and pink child's backpack rested on the table next to it, and a set of keys hung off one side.

Donovan turned the bag around and raised the keys. "It's Gina's; I can tell by this button," a 'Hello Kitty' button pin, hung off one side. He looked inside, pulled out two books with brown bag covers, two notebooks, a pen, and a pencil case, 'Hello Kitty,' and laid them out on the table. He then opens the bag fully, showing it to O'Malley, nothing more.

O'Malley noticed a shipping label on the box and the address label was for Donovan at his old address, at MacBride's house: 467 Ash Dr. O'Malley used his pen to open the box more and pulled out a long white and black gloves. "Looks like all the missing formal gloves."

"Have Mac's team bag and tag all this for prints and trace," Donovan said turning back and walking out. MacBride, Duke, and Stein were waiting, with MacBride leaning on Duke. The camera crew records MacBride moving from Duke to Donovan, still distraught and dropped to the ground. Donovan saw the crew and pointed, Duke quickly ran up, and placed his hand on the camera, trying to cover MacBride's pain, "Any comments for our viewers, Sergeant Dubcek?"

O'Malley's slowly rolled up in front of the old biker's bar, old as if they had never remolded or cleaned since the early eighties. Old furniture, bikes, beer cans, kegs, and bike parts were flung all over. There were about ten bikers, from eighteen to late fifties sitting around, lying around on the furniture, or their bikes, and looking as if they had one hell of a blowout the night before. Most were wearing blue jeans, white T-shirts, or long-sleeved flannel shirts, and most were wearing black vests, their "cuts," some with patches on the front, their rocker on the back, and at the bottom. 'North Mammoth,' a medieval knight with a helmet shield up, with a skull face and riding a bike in the center of the cuts, coming toward them, with a staff and flag. A coat of arms, a field of white with three blue Fleurs-de-lis, a green field on the bottom, and red along the top with a screaming eagle.

Donovan stepped out of the SUV and leaned back in toward O'Malley, who was eating an oversized pastrami sandwich, with heavy mustard, and he was very messy. "You are joining us?"

"No, I am fine right here," he said picking at the sandwich and his shirt.

Donovan nodded, as he heard the back passenger door slam shut, "Always knew you would have my six, Master Sergeant," he said to Stein without turning around.

"On your six, Commander," Stein answered.

Donovan nodded to O'Malley who was still picking the sandwich off his shirt and trying to clean off the mustard stains. Slowly they walked through the minefield of parts and people, some still sleeping and some waking. Watching as the others, knowing they were the ones out of place, a kid jumped in front of him, out of nowhere, no more than sixteen, a 'hang around,' lowest of lows within the motorcycle club, a wannabe, and has not yet earned his cuts. A tall kid, towering over

Donovan, who himself was nearly six-foot-tall, looked up at the kid, then out of the corner of his eye, and saw an old biker looking at him, watching them. White, mid-sixties, 'Vice President,' stitched into his cuts, he sat on his old-style oversized Indian bike, looking over his sunglasses, from under his brown tattered cowboy hat, long gray hair, ponytail, and bushy goatee, waiting to see who moved first, the kid or Donovan. Something about the old biker looked familiar to him, but he could not place him.

"You're not welcome here!" The kid yelled.

Donovan looked back over his shoulder toward Stein, and then quickly at the old biker, again. Then with both arms and all his strength, he shoved the kid back, slamming the kid, sailing him back across the lot and through the bar's front door. A four-by-four-window pane on top and he continued through. The crash woke the other bikers, who took positions around Donovan and Stein, grabbing pipes, glass shards, and knives, all ready for a fight. But the old biker on his oversized Indian bike cleared his throat and pushed his hat down over his face. They took it as a sign to let it go, leave him alone, and let him get on with his business.

The kid continued across the room and skidded into the jukebox, cutting the country music off. A large, oversized man in his late forties, 'President,' stitched into his front cuts, brown-slicked back hair pulled back into a long ponytail, thick scruffy beard, with some gray along his chin, slammed his beer down, stood up with a few others, and slowly walked up to Donovan, limping and straightening his cuts.

With a Cheshire cat smile on her face, the mature Asian woman with him shifted in her chair wearing blue jean shorts and a top. They continued slowly and walked in through, hearing catcalls, whistles, and howls ring out toward Stein, she opened her jacket slowly revealing her shield on her waistband, and the noise stopped. The large man stepped in front of Donovan, cutting his path off, looking him over, and then grabbed him in a huge bear hug, lifting him off the floor. Stein looked closely at the man, with curiosity that she knew him.

"Donny ol' boy, how the hell are you!" the large biker said.

"Good," as he cleared his throat and caught his breath again. "Master Sergeant Stein, seventh division, May I introduce, my old friend Gunnery Sergeant Angus O'Malley, ninth division." Stein now fully realized, and he had read her file, and now realized the family resemblance.

The gang let out a loud roar of laughter, after hearing Donovan call him Angus, but Angus gave out a louder yell as the alpha male stopped them, and each returned to their own business. Angus snapped to attention and saluted Stein, "My pleasure, Master Sergeant," he then waved them toward the bar, slamming his fists down, "Three beers, Cookie?" A very young, dark-haired Asian girl stepped up with three long-neck beers, wearing blue jean shorts, and a jacket like the other Asian woman. She could not be a day over sixteen, Donovan thought. Angus saw the look on Donovan's face, and slapped him on the shoulder, "Trust me, old friend, she's twenty-one, legal as the day is long."

She smiled at Donovan, "Who's your friend, Daddy?"

Angus let out a deep belly laugh, "This is the ol' boy I told you and your Momma about. If it was not for him, I'd be dead three times over."

"And I thought you saved men three times over, Angus," Donovan replied as he sipped the beer. Looking back at Stein, and the gang laughed again. Angus looked around with disgust, and then leaned over near Donovan, and whispered, "Please don't call me that here, it's Poppa Bear, please."

Stein took a drink as the tall lengthy blonde biker stepped up as if sniffing her. She swung her left fist back, hard and fast, in one motion, knocking him out.

"I am calling in a marker, Poppa Bear, I need your help," Donovan said, looking at him with a bit of confusion in his eyes.

Angus was taken back a bit, drunk some of his beer, and laughed. He picked up Donovan's right hand, showing him his palm, "You have the whole, Jackson Hole Sheriff's department under this, and you need my help, Donny ol' boy?"

"True, but what I need, cannot be on the books," Donovan said, as he turned some toward the larger man.

Angus stepped back with stretched-out arms as if introducing the gang as his own, "What can I do for my oldest and dearest friend?"

Donovan shifted around on the stool toward him, "You have heard of the serial killer?"

Papa Bear spat on the floor. "Yes, the damn coward!"

"She has my girls."

Angus looked at the floor, a few sighs from the women and groans from the men in the bar, most of the gang knew Donovan, MacBride, and the girl, in this small town.

"Female, you say?" The mature Asian woman who was sitting next to Angus stepped up. "And she has your girls. Name it, cous."

Stein nearly spilled her beer, sipping more upon hearing her say 'cous.' Angus was again taken aback by one of his ladies, which was not normal to speak about club business with a nonmember, or even talk in front of the women, or over Poppa Bear's authority. She was different. Poppa Bear and Donovan both knew her history: her mother and she were able to emigrate from Vietnam to America with some help from Donovan's Father. She was like an aunt or cousin to him.

"Thanks, Mai. Yesterday, we got word from Jock. I wish to ask since you all know this town and have an ear and hand in everything."

She hugged him, and Stein shifted around toward them, watched the family's concern, and thought. Who does he not know in this town?

"You never…." Mai started, but Angus stepped up cutting her off.

"Yes, you never have to ask."

"Anything you can learn or hear, let me know?" Donovan said as he put the bottle down on the bar and turned to leave.

Angus slapped his old friend on his shoulder, again. "Yes, Donny ol' boy!"

Donovan turned, Stein followed, and kept watch on the bar. As they reached the pool table near the front, the lengthy blonde biker regained consciousness and stood slowly, and she decked him again.

"Sorry about the 'hang around,'" Donovan yelled back, heard Angus's loud belly laugh, and climbed into the SUV. He looked back one last time, over at the old biker on the old oversized Indian bike, who looked back at him. Hoping the others did not see, he saluted and laughed. Donovan still couldn't place the old biker, but the salute, very military, and the laugh struck a nerve somewhere in his childhood.

"How's Angus?" O'Malley asked, Stein finally saw the resemblance, with his bad black hair dye job, and clean-shaven face.

"Good. Ferg and the others will keep a lookout," Donovan said as he waved him on.

"You know, I can't stand that old bastard," O'Malley replied.

"I know, I know, but you could have at least said hello to your sister-in-law and niece," Donovan said as Stein held back her laughter with a half-smile.

"Have something to say, partner?" O'Malley asked with a smile, seeing her in the rear-view mirror.

She was trying hard to hold back her laughter, and finally saw it in O'Malley's face. They're twins. "No partner, all good."

"Where to now?" O'Malley asked.

"Roadhouse Grill, I need to check in on Sarah. She's with Jock now," Donovan said as he put his seatbelt on.

The SUV slowly backed out and Duke called out over the radio, "Moj Bratanek, have your ears on?"

"Go, Wujek."

"I wish you two would talk English," O'Malley said with irritation.

"I find Polish a lovely language, just an Uncle and Nephew conversing," Stein replied.

"Two more," Duke informed them.

"My Girls?"

"No, thank god. We're at the Sherman Heritage Museum." Duke replied over the radio.

"On our way!" Donovan said as O'Malley flipped on the lights, and they sped off. Donovan kept his eyes on the old biker.

Angus, outside now, and standing with the old biker on his oversized Indian bike, "Know why he was here?"

"Probably needing some help."

"Yes, the town's Serial Killer has his girls."

The old biker fell back into his oversized bike, still watching the SUV driving off. "Whatever he needs, will be there for him, right?"

"Your call, he's family."

The old Biker stood, started his oversized Indian bike, and sped off. "I'll let you know, Angus."

The room was dark except for a single light coming from a small four-by-four window, about eight feet up in the wall. The room was cold. Robin sat up, still wearing her uniform from the Pearl Drop club, her head was pounding from whatever she was hit with. She tried to stand but fell back against the wall because her left arm was chained to the floor. She could tell the room was very old with dust in the air, and cobwebs near the ceiling. She felt pain coursing through her lower back. She reached around, ran her hand along her lower back, and pulled it back fast. Blood and green ink covered her hand, she tried to look over her shoulder.

"Don't worry, bitch! The ink and blood will dry soon, and then the whole world will know my newest lil plaything," Jacquelyn said. She stood in black leather pants, black knee-high boots, topless, her large breast hanging out, and wearing a very long, thick black strap-on, and four inches around.

"What you going to do to me?" Robin asked with fright.

"Enjoy you," she laughed. "Strip bitch! And get on all fours." Robin screamed. Jacquelyn laughed again. "Scream all you want, no one cares. Whoever is upstairs will just enjoy it. Now strip, bitch!"

Robin moved back against the wall, shaking from the cold and fright. Jacquelyn cracked a bullwhip, she was holding in her left hand. Slowly, Robin undid her tie and blouse, slipped it off, and let it fall, dangling on the chain, then she removed her bra, and let it drop to the floor, exposing her small breast, and large areolas. Jacquelyn smiled with delight, licking her lips, and enjoying the show. Robin removed each of her boots and tossed one at her, but she moved out of the way. "Now, now, plaything."

Jacquelyn waved her to continue. Robin started to cry as she undid her skirt and let it drop—no panties. "Oh yea, what a nice cute clean cunt. Now get on all fours, facing away, bitch!" Jacquelyn ordered and motioned with the bullwhip and waited.

Crying more with hiccups, she turned around slowly, but kept her eyes on her. "What … you are going … to do to me?"

"Fuck you like you have never been fucked before, Bitch. Unlike you, the staff is not allowed to play with the clients, so I am going to enjoy you for all the staff." Jacquelyn said moving closer.

"I am staff, just like you!"

"Whore!" she yelled and laughed. She cracked the whip on her ass, and Robin jumped, "You may screen people for Ms. Amanda, and help with special guests and events, but I know you have been Ms. Amanda's personal bitch, and fucktoy for some time now. You fucking cunt whore!" She told her as she placed her long think trap-on, on her backside, and grabbed her hips hard.

Robin let out a loud painful cry and collapsed. Jacquelyn grabbed her tighter and then looked over at the two dresses, white and black, which are hanging on a shelf unit next to her, pondering which one she will choose for her.

"Are you enjoying your little playthings, princess?" Old Lady Sherman called down from upstairs.

"Oh yes, grandmother. I am enjoying all my lil slut whores." She answered and stood up.

"Good girl. Now you play nicely with them. Your Momma and I have a few young ones ourselves upstairs, we are entertaining. If you get bored with yours, come on up, and join us, the more the merrier." Old Lady Sherman said and then closed the cellar door.

"Yes Ma'am, I will keep that in mind." She answered and turned around to the shelf unit behind her, picking up a long, yellow-blade serrated hacksaw, with a few paint chips missing on the blade, next to a tray with many teardrop pearl necklaces. She turned back toward Robin, then over to the far side of the room, where two metal surgical tables sat, she walked over to the first one, a young girl, maybe eighteen, nude, in restraints, she was waking, and started to struggle. On the other table, another teen girl, unconscious and lying on her belly, there was an inking machine for tattooing next to the table and both had red hair.

Jacquelyn stepped up to the first girl and caressed her hair, then pinched her young puffy nipples, the girl mumbled and yelled something through the red ball gag in her mouth, with tears and fright in her eyes. "Hush, now baby girl. Mommy is not done with you, my lil plaything." Jacquelyn said as she showed her the saw, and she jumped back. "Let us try this again, are you now going to be a good lil baby girl for Mommy, and not fight her again?"

The girl shivered at the sight of the saw and nodded and mumbled through her ball gag. "Yes, Mommy."

She laid the saw on a metal table to her left, next to a basin full of water and a few left hands. She climbed up on the table, on top of the girl, parting her legs, kissing her, and rocking back and forth.

The girl turned her head to the side, crying, closing her eyes, and hearing, "Yes, you are a good baby girl, for Mommy."

The SUV came to a screeching stop outside the museum. Duke waited at the entrance, and Roberts and her teams were already inside. McKnight's Lincoln was outside; a female deputy raised the tape, and Duke waved them to follow him. The old biker pulled up slowly on his oversized Indian bike and stopped behind the Lincoln, watching along with others in the crowd behind the tapeline. Camille and her crew, and other TV vans pulled up, setting up behind the tape, and the old biker drove off.

"How old and where are they?" Donovan asked, putting on gloves.

"Second floor, Civil War display, and both early twenties," Duke explained as he led them in. "Alice, Richard, and their teams were already working, collecting samples, marking the scene, getting castings, and looking over the bodies. They're different this time, there nude."

McKnight came from an alcove and stepped in line with them as they neared the scene. "Why nude, Donovan?"

"Alice will find a lot more differences now. She's devolving, losing control. Now that we have Grant, she knows we are on to her. She feels she no longer has the time to enjoy them after using them and just discards them when done and finds new ones," Donovan explained.

"Yes, and I get that, but why nude?" McKnight asked again.

"She does not care anymore. She just enjoys them, and tossing them, like you would a beer can." Donovan answered.

"Yes, very sloppy. No makeup, very abusive around the genitals, and cuts along the legs and belly, and all hands present. She was keeping hands as trophies and now keeps them fresh with alcohol, especially on the cuts," Roberts said as she pointed at different places on the bodies, as Donovan and the rest of the team join her.

"Why here?" The old Sheriff asked, and now in a blue suit, coming from the far end of the wing with the curator of the museum, an old man in his sixties and very British, wearing a black tuxedo.

"It will take months to clean this up," the Curator complained.

"She is still telling you to look at the Sherman's, again," the old Sheriff commented.

"Yes, and we'll be serving warrants soon on the old homestead," Donovan said, turning toward him.

"Be careful, son. Your daddy tried that and got himself killed," The old Sheriff explained with stern eyes.

Donovan nodded, stooped down toward the bodies, and looked them over, and the scene. "Anything else out of the ordinary?"

"A Stiletto footprint," Roberts said, pointing to an area near one of the girl's feet where Duke was next to Donovan, where a ruler card sat, waiting for casting.

"I'd say a knee-high Stiletto boot, from the shape of the toe imprint," Stein commented as Roberts smiled up at her. "I have a pair like these."

"And?" Donovan said.

"This …" Roberts said as she handed Donovan a large evidence bag, with a medium-sized black day planner. "I found this under her," she pointed at the girl on her right.

"Interesting. Find anything inside, useful?" Donovan asked, looking at it but not taking it.

"Yes, she's a lesbian escort," Roberts commented, the Sheriff, rolled his eyes, not believing, a 'Lesbian escort,' in his town. "And very prominent in the town. I found many female names, dates, and times for meetings. She had three hours blocked out tomorrow at two p.m., with Ms. Amanda, at the Pearl Drop Club. I tagged it for you," Roberts explained.

Donovan took it and handed it to Stein. "Return this to my office." Donovan stepped over to the Curator and the Sheriff. "Mr. Curator? Do you know either of these girls?"

"No!" The Curator said strongly with embarrassment. "And could you please cover them up?"

"Soon. Have you ever seen them here?" Donovan asked.

"No!" The Curator said, turning around. "Please cover them up!"

The Sheriff walked Donovan off a bit from the crime scene. "How is Sarah? And have you had any word on your girls?"

"Better than I thought she would, was going to check on her when Duke called this in. Nothing yet on my girls," Donovan said, as he scanned over the reaming of the room and exhibits, not really wishing to talk with this man.

"You go, be with Sarah. I know Alice and O'Malley have this," the Sheriff said trying to be a friend or mentor.

"Yeah… soon…" Donovan started to say, then saw a display of blue and gray soldiers, out the corner of his eye, each officer, and both Captains, but the gray was an African American mannequin, "Have you ever seen a black confederate officer, Sheriff?"

The Curator turned fast and ran at the display, but Donovan stopped him, and two deputies held him back. "Hold him." Donovan walked over to the display, looking it over, especially the face of the black one, and then turned back at Roberts. "May I borrow your black light, Alice, please?"

Roberts stood and reached into her large kit, pulled out a three-foot-long fluorescent bulb encased in a small black case, and handed, it over to Donovan, he turned it on and waved it slowly over the black silk face. Letters illuminated: 'If at first you don't succeed. Try, try again.'

"She's laughing at you," Roberts said.

"Yes." and then he ran it over the white silk-faced mannequin. "I have two, next I'll have three."

"Who's the third?" Roberts asked with concern in her voice.

"I think she is telling me she'll go after Sarah next, or that she is making me one of her playthings, by doing her bidding," Donovan answered.

"How did you know to look here?" Roberts asked as she took her light back.

"Her family is known for her Great-grandfather being a Major in the Civil War alongside his namesake, the General. She knew this black Confederate officer would stick out to me. As we learn more about her, she is learning more about me, and knows I enjoy American History, and both our families fought in the Civil War. A Black Confederate officer would stick out, and then I saw some liquid on the faces. Let him go." Donovan explained as he waved toward the two deputies, holding the curator. "I am sorry, Dr. Curator. We will be taking these too."

"My name is Dr. Watson. Not Mr. Curator!" The Curator said with a very stern voice.

McKnight handed Donovan a sheet of paper, he was given by a female team member, a brunette in a gray business suit, who hurried in and handed it to Donovan, who scanned it over. "How did you get the DNA back so fast?"

"With all the shit out of left field, I thought you'd need it fast," McKnight explained.

"Thanks."

Grant was still in the cell, sitting, cuffed, and in an orange jumpsuit. He looked up at Donovan. "You may not be the killer, but I do know you're related to her and taught her a thing or two, medically and surgically."

Grant laughed, "How the fuck am I related to that fucking dyke whore?"

"You're Sister!" Donovan yelled back, holding the DNA report up.

"Like you think I know the answers, you're the gumshoe! But I know you're going to tell me anyway," Grant said, not looking at him.

"I don't think you were married, common law or otherwise."

Grant laughed louder, "You think I made it all up?"

"Yes, to hide the fact and make the story of a husband more believable. You are the incestuous son of the Mother and the late Grandfather," Donovan said coldly holding the DNA report inside the bars, for him to see, knowing he could read the DNA results. "As well as the brother of my serial killer, who is also from the same incestuous relationship. I'd bet a month's pay on that. We ran your DNA," Donovan said, letting the report drop to the floor.

"Why the hell do you think I would help that bitch, sister or not?" Grant said, standing up.

"Because I know you already have. How the family treated you both, disowning you after years of abuse before puberty, and how the women enjoy the women in that family. You want to get back at good ol' Granny as much as she does, that's why she has been pointing me at the family," Donovan explained.

Grant dropped down onto the bunk. "Now you think I am going to help you stop her."

"No, but with your surgical skills, and all you taught her, I know you helped her dump the bodies, in the forest and cemetery. We had a witness," Grant shot him a look. "Yes, we also found DNA and traces from the forest and the cemetery. I have enough to lock you up as an accessory for life, maybe even for the death penalty," Donovan explained as he started to leave.

"I know where she is. I want a deal!" Grant said, quickly moving toward the bars.

Donovan stopped, turned back slowly, choosing his words carefully, "And what could you have that could help me? I would need more than her location and your confession of the body dumps and surgical skills you gave her."

Grant looked up at Donovan, knowing he only had one last chance, but he was screwed either way, by him or the old lady. Donovan turned, and the guard opened the door. "I know the combinations to the private rooms in the Mansion, where they have been keeping the little girls they have been abducting over the years and abusing. I know that house like the back of my hand." Grant yelled, showing the back of his hands, the best he could with the cuffs behind him. Donovan looked down, wondering if this was another game.

Maria let out a chilling scream from upstairs. The menacing biker stood over seven and a half feet tall, with three surgical scars cut into his right cheek from facial reconstruction surgery, and his left eye only partly open. He had no hair except a single black streak from the top down the back, like a short bushy Mohawk. He was dragging his right leg toward Stein, who was sitting at her desk. He remembered her from the bar, 'Treasurer,' stitched on his cuts, she looked up with shock seeing him. Maria was shaking and hiding behind Duke and a few other deputies near the check-in desk.

O'Malley jumped to his feet, pulled his gun, aiming it at the tall, towering beast, as Donovan entered and placed his hand on the barrel, and slowly lowered it, "Heal, Frankenstein," Donovan ordered, the biker stopped, turned slowly toward Donovan's voice, and growled. Stein quickly moved back behind Donovan, Duke shifted across from Donovan, and behind Frankenstein.

"What the fuck is that?" Stein whimpered to Donovan.

Donovan walked over to Frankenstein, and patted him on his shoulder, "This is Frankenstein, a fellow Marine, Master Sergeant, Angus, and I served with in Fallujah. His legs and right arm, which have been re-attached so many times and his face put back together, we call him, Frankenstein."

Frankenstein reached into his back pocket, and the deputies pulled out their guns and aimed. Donovan put his arms out and up, "Stand down, that's an order. Stand down!" Lowering their guns but keeping an eye on Frankenstein. He handed him a small piece of paper to Donovan.

"Poppa Bear, there," Frankenstein says in a deep, sharp, gravelly voice. Then turned slowly and limps out. The deputies raised their guns again, and Donovan puts his hands back up.

O'Malley reads over Donovan's shoulder, "What's that?"

"Poppa Bear found girls, warehouse in the old cannery district, five men holding them," Frankenstein said.

"Saddle up, Duke, full tactical gear!" Donovan ordered.

Duke ran toward the stairs, pointing out ten deputies. Donovan and O'Malley followed, and Stein ran out the front.

Just before sunrise, Angus and the old biker were waiting, sitting on their bikes in front of the old building in the cannery district. Angus on an early sixties Harley, as two armored trucks raced up followed by O'Malley's SUV. Duke and the boys hurried out, all in SWAT gear. Duke, was the only one of the three wearing a face shield. The other deputies exited the armored trucks, also in SWAT gear, and took positions near the building. Donovan stepped up to Angus, as O'Malley confirmed sniper position on the building across the street with Duke, who ran off with the two drivers of the trucks, both with rifles, as Donovan's sixty-six Corvette raced in, squealing to a stop, nearly slamming into one of the armored trucks.

Donovan turned as he heard the squealing tires of his classic Corvette, and the old biker stood up over his oversized Indian bike. "Fuck!" he yelled as he saw the priceless possession about to be destroyed for no reason.

"What we got?" Donovan asked Angus.

"There are five on the third floor, halfway up, and two in the back, near the loading docks, with the girls," The old biker said.

Donovan thought, looking up and over the building, then turned back to Angus. "Sheikh's gambit. . ."

Angus nodded and yelled, "We're out of here!" and the old biker followed.

MacBride exited his sixty-six Corvette on the driver's side and ran up to Donovan. "They in there?"

"Yes!"

Very frantic, "Get 'em out of there!"

"Angus and I have a plan, we used in Fallujah when we had to rescue a Sheik's daughter," she flashed a stern look. "Go back to the car with Stein. Trust me, it will be ok, we will all walk away from this, including the girls." Donovan tapped his mic on his shoulder twice, "Duke, ready?"

"Give the word, L.T."

He waved his hand up in a circle, and O'Malley stepped back and moved up to Donovan near the team at the entrance.

"Look here!" An African American boy dressed in black in his twenties with dreads called out. An older African American man bald in his fifties comes up fast from the rear, also in black, and looks out the window where the boy is pointing.

"We set?" The man asked as they saw Donovan's team crash through the doors with battering rams and entering the building.

"Yeah," The boy answered, the two men moved off back into the dark. Two small metal canisters came crashing through the window landing on the floor, with a flash of bright light and smoke filling the room. The two scurry out followed by three others also in black and ski masks.

Donovan took off after the young boy up a set of stairs, two higher levels, and down a long corridor, into a room with five computer screens, showing the outside and his girls in the back somewhere. The boy tapped three buttons on the keyboard as Donovan came running in, tackling him. Two other SWAT team members enter each wearing gas masks. Donovan rolled off of him. "Hold him!"

They grabbed him, placed him on his knees, and held hands behind his head, "You're too late!" he yelled.

Donovan turned slowly toward the screens, the center one changed from his girls to a digital clock, 15:00 ~~ 59, 58, 57...

"Move!" Donovan yelled.

MacBride watched and waited, she and Stein heard the explosion, glass, and a fireball exited the windows from near the top floor. Stein pulled MacBride into one of the armored trucks, as O'Malley exited with the bulk of the team and four of the hostage takers. The two SWAT team members that were with Donovan followed with the young boy, as the building imploded.

MacBride watched from a window inside the armored truck, as the building collapsed, smoke, dust, and debris everywhere. "Donovan!" she yelled with tears down her face from the horror.

Survivors

Robin awoke to muffled screams, still naked and lying on the cold floor, shivering from the cold night air, with a collar around her neck – a silver metal collar with a small red bulb in front. With another scream, she could tell where the scream was coming from; Jacquelyn was now topless and kneeling on top of one of the metal tables across the room, and she could barely make out the other female body underneath her in the darkness. Jacquelyn was cutting her along her thighs and belly, and after each cut, she placed a small towel over the cut to control the bleeding.

"Did you get some sleep, bitch? I am far from done with you," Jacquelyn said, jumping off the table and grabbing a set of black sweats and a large flowery comforter, and tossing them at her. Robin grabbed them and pulled the comforter tight to her body like a sleeping bag, trying to keep warm. "Get dressed! I need you alive to help me."

She pulled the sweatpants on and grabbed the top. "I will never help you, bitch!"

Jacquelyn smiled and pulled a small black device from her jeans, a white button on one side. She pressed it, and a red light on top flashed, and the red light on the collar flashed as well. Robin shook feverishly and fell over. "I said, get dressed, Bitch! You're going to help me!"

"No!"

Jacquelyn pressed it again, and she shook again, landing on the floor, passed out again. "In time, Bitch." She grabbed and put on her grey sweatshirt, sleeveless and slit down each side, and walked over to the table with the second girl, who had started moaning and was still on her belly.

Jacquelyn ran her fingertips over the fresh tattoo on the young girl's lower back and heard her moan. She quickly turned her over to their twins, tapped on the white ball gag still in her mouth, and tied her down to the table quickly, by her wrists and ankles with blue nylon rope, each three feet in length. Then she caressed her red hair and looked over her young nude body, slowly running her hand down along her face, over her shoulders, and down around both her breasts. "Yes, lovely, and so nice. I will enjoy you so much."

She opened her eyes and with shock saw Jacquelyn standing over her, feeling the gag in her mouth and the restraints, jumped, struggling against them. She caressed her face gently. "Hush, baby girl. Mommy is going to enjoy you, as much as I enjoyed your sister," Jacquelyn said, looking back at the first girl.

The girl tried to scream, but was muffled by the gag, and continued to fight. Jacquelyn picked up a large metal pipe about two feet long from the table with the inking machine and slammed it against the surgical table. The girl froze, looking at her. The girl on the other table jumped and screamed upon hearing the metal pipe hitting the table. Robin woke up from hearing it also. Jacquelyn moved back over toward Robin, stooping down, and taking her chin tightly. "Now, my lil bitch?" as she held the device up to her face. "You will be a good girl for Mommy?"

Robin nodded quickly with fear, trying to pull away. Jacquelyn kissed her harshly and then tossed her aside like a rag doll. "Finish dressing, Bitch! Mommy has a lot of errands to finish, and it is time to find Mommy two more baby girls and time to finish my plans with Donovan, specifically his beautiful wife Sarah."

Shock flooded Robin's face. She quickly finished dressing, pulled the comforter over her again, and cowered back against the wall. Jacquelyn headed back over to the second girl, running her hand down her shoulders, over her belly, and down between her legs, parting them. "Yes, very lovely. Mommy likes," the girl shook from her touching, trying to pull away but could not.

A woman in her fifties, with dark black hair, nude with large sagging breasts, pea-shaped nipples, and large areolas, with a large black and gray shaggy unkempt bush. With a leather collar around her neck, with a single loop in front, and looking very used, with a large fresh red handprint on her left cheek slowly climbed down the stairs and said, "Honey, Grandmother wishes to talk with you."

Jacquelyn turned fast, picking a knife up off the inking table, small, with a blade less than two-inch blade, and a four-inch black handle identical to the one she was using on the first girl. "Mother, I have told you not to interrupt me when I am playing with my baby girls!"

The girls on the table started yelling and moving to get her attention. Jacquelyn took the blade and stabbed it into the girl's right upper arm. "Fine, Mother!" the girl screamed, and Jacquelyn walked back over to Robin and put the chain back on her left wrist. "Are you going to be a good girl for Mommy and stay put?" Robin nodded. Jacquelyn took a black leather collar from the four-by-four posts near the staircase and put it around her neck. She removed her top and jeans, kicking off her flats. "Nude, as Grandmother requires us," she said, with her hands out to show herself off. Her Mother nodded and started back up the stairs.

Jacquelyn straightened up, like her Mother, lowered her eyes, and followed her up the stairs.

They heard the door slam closed, the two girls look at Robin, who stood trying to stretch over to them and looked up the stairs. She was not even halfway across the room. She tried to reach for the table with the hacksaw, but was unable to reach it, either. She returned to the wall and pulled on the chain, hoping to rip it from the wall. Robin pushed against the wall with her leg, but it was no use. She stretched out to the far wall, which had the two dresses, stretching with her fingertips barely reaching the ledge. The girls were in awe of what she was doing and prayed she would make it.

The door upstairs opened. "Grandmother, please. I have my *own* baby girls. You always told us, they come first," She slammed the door. Robin jumped back and returned to the wall and covered up. Jacquelyn took the collar off and placed it back on the post. Dressed and looked over at Robin, then pulled the knife out of the girl's shoulder. She screamed, and blood flowed. She grabbed a towel from the bin on the table and placed it on the cut, holding it tight, looking up at the ceiling. "Mother, see what you made me do to my baby girl. I didn't wish to hurt them. It will be ok baby; Mommy will take care of you."

"Shoes?" Robin asked quietly, almost in a whisper.

"Oh, yes, I forgot. Need to look good when you're out, with Mommy," she said and reached down under the table and pulled out black stilettos with two-inch heels, and tossed them.

"Heels and sweats?" Robin asked. Jacquelyn took out the device and showed it to her, tapping the button but not pushing it. "Yes, Mommy. Thank you, Mommy."

Jacquelyn picked up two syringes that were lying on the inking table, looked at them, pushed some of the liquid out, and jabbed it into each of the girls' arms and they quickly fell asleep. She tossed a key from her other pocket. "Stand up," she ordered, still holding the device. "Unlock yourself."

Robin grabbed the key quickly from the floor next to her. "Good girl. Please place those blankets on the girls." Robin walked over slowly to the second girl and saw a thick black blanket, neatly folded on the edge of the table under her feet and covered the girl. She moved to the first girl, picked up the blanket, and shifted a bit, hoping not to be seen, and pulled a small jagged file out from inside her cuff, she had gotten off the shelf before Jacquelyn returned from upstairs. She placed it under the blanket in the girl's hand and turned back toward Jacquelyn.

Jacquelyn waved at her with one finger, and Robin slowly walked back. She patted her head softly. "Good girl, let us go now. Mommy has errands to run," Jacqueline said as she pointed to an area behind the shelving unit near the back of the room. They walked around it and up a small ramp that was cut into the wall. Jacquelyn pushed the double doors of the cellar and opened it, letting the bright sunlight in. It was early morning, and Robin shielded her eyes.

The tan 'Econoline' van sat right at the back door of the cellar. "Drive!" and tossed her the keys.

"Where are we going?" Robin asked, looking around to try and find out where she was.

"Not your concern, Bitch. Drive!" she said as they climbed into the van and drove off down the long dirt road and out of the Sherman Estate, through the open gate onto the blacktop, and onto the main road into town.

"Take this road for about ten minutes, then you will know where you are, and then we are going to the Pear Drop Club."

"You said, Sarah?"

"Yes, I did. I know she is at the club, informing Ms. Amanda of Donovan's death. Two birds with one stone," Jacquelyn said, laughing.

Shocked, "Dead?" Robin asked.

"Just drive, Bitch," Jackyln ordered, holding the device where she could see it.

Poppa Bear and the old Biker slowly work their way up into the loading dock. Poppa Bear holding a .45 pistol, and the old Biker with a three-fifty-seven long barrel magnum. The old Biker waved Poppa Bear to a door as he saw a shadow crossing through the window of the door, each stood on either side of the swinging double doors. Poppa Bear looked through the small window, seeing an African American man in his late twenties looking back through the window, taking the door edge with his hand, and slamming it into the man's face. Then pulled the door toward him, the young man fell forward, and the old Biker caught him, placed a bandana in his mouth, laid him gently on the floor, tied his hands behind his back with a bandana from Poppa Bear, and put him behind a stack of boxes off to the side. Poppa Bear waved at him with his gun to continue in. Poppa Bear went right, and the old Biker went left, as the door closed slowly.

Poppa Bear turned a corner, seeing the girls on two cots. Marci still in her black skirt and hoodie. Gina has red hair like her Mother's also, and is in a white dress, combing her little doll's hair. She looked up and saw him, and starts to yell, toward Pappa Bear, but he puts his hand up to stop her. The old Biker knocked the other older African American man out, who was facing the girls. Gina ran to Poppa Bear, calling out to him, and he put his hand over her mouth. The old biker grabbed Marci as they ran out, the way Poppa Bear entered, back out the loading dock and across the street, behind a twenty-foot concrete wall, as the building implodes.

Gina grabbed Poppa Bear tight, and held onto the old Biker, as dust and derbies flew over their heads. They heard MacBride yelling for Donovan off in the distance, on the other side of the building.

"We're out of here!" the old Biker yelled as he picked up Marci and got on his bike. She held onto him tightly. Gina held on to her dolly and Poppa Bear on his Harley, and they all rode off.

The building was in rubble, with smoke and dust still hanging in the air. MacBride looked out the window of the armored truck at what was left of the entrance and ran. Duke and O'Malley grabbed her and held her back. She dropped to her knees, crying, "Donovan, my girls, my girls!"

Stein grabbed her and sat down next to her. "I know he got them out."

O'Malley looked down at them. "I know my Brother got the girls out," both trying to comfort her, knowing she was lost now. She held Stein, crying and calling for her girls.

Duke waved to a few of the deputies that had joined them. "Rope it off! Six-block radius," and then joined O'Malley with the hostage takers. "How much did she pay you to kill my Nephew?" he yelled at him as he grabbed the older man by the collar and pulled him up.

O'Malley pulled Duke off, as two SWAT officers pushed the man back to the ground. "Duke, take it easy. This is not how T would want it."

"If he is dead ,O'Malley, that bitch is...."

"It was not a woman that paid us," the young boy blurted out.

"Shut up!" the old man yelled, slamming into him.

"Separate them!" O'Malley yelled, pulling the boy up and slamming him into the armored truck. "Then who?" The boy laughed, and O'Malley slammed his fist into the boy's belly.

Duke put his hand on O'Malley's shoulder. "Ferg?"

"This is what T would accept. Now, who paid you if not a woman?"

The boy took a deep breath. "Your boss!"

"Donovan is *my* boss," Duke said.

Laughing, "No, no, the Sheriff paid us fifty thousand dollars to slow him down. He told us to take the girls."

"Why?" Duke asked.

"You know. You were there thirty years ago, and helped with the cover-up," the older man yelled from the group.

O'Malley shot a look at Duke, not understanding what the boy had said, as two deputies took him.

Duke ran a few feet, rubbing his hands, damning himself under his breath, and kicking at the ground, knowing it was his fault.

O'Malley stopped him. "What's he talking about, Duke?"

"Thirty years ago, when Malachi ran a similar case against the Shermans and their… their sinful acts, the county, the council, and the new sheriff, the Captain then, closed the books, covered it up, after Malachi's murder, and shredded most of it."

"The sheriff killed T and my girls, and you knew about it?" MacBride slapped him, crying and hitting him.

Duke pulled her tight, "I am so sorry, Sarah," turned and handed his shield and gun to O'Malley."

"You started this shit. You're going to finish it for the girls' sake!" O'Malley said, refusing the shield and gun.

Hanson and Scott were driving their patrol route, and she pointed ahead of them. He looked up and saw two figures in blankets walking, holding onto each other. He tapped his siren twice, and one of the girls dropped to the ground, the other caught her and turned, and they could see they were nude. They quickly stopped and ran up to them, "She had you!" Scott yelled.

The one still somewhat standing nodded. Scott ran to the back of the squad car for more blankets.

"Base, this is Hanson. Inform Donovan we have two survivors, and we need a bus at Crenshaw and Main, hurry," Hanson reported as people started running up to see, but Hanson motioned them back.

"Bus on its way, Donovan listed… dead," O'Malley replied on the radio. Both looked at each other in shock.

"Check," Hanson answered.

O'Malley pulled up with Stein, the scene was taped off, and the girls were now in the ambulance, still holding each other tight, "What you got?" O'Malley asked as Stein climbed in next to the girls.

"We clear?" The paramedic asked, and Hanson waved him off. He closed the doors, slapped the ambulance twice, and ran around to the front as it sped off, lights and sirens ringing out.

"The Morgan Sisters, seniors at Hamilton High. One was able to give me some facts. They were grabbed at the movie theater, not sure when, but from what the medics could see, it's bad," Hanson explained while reviewing his notes.

"They're Alive!" O'Malley corrected him.

"They say a girl, Robin, they knew her as one of the staffers at the Pear Drop club and is being forced to do things. Robin was able to get a knife so the girls could cut themselves free after they woke up from a needle shot.

Watching the ambulance speed off, "They're alive, and some good leads for Donovan if he was still with us. Contact Alice, have her get to the hospital, and get Mac and his team here. ABP out on Robin from the club and make sure everyone knows Robin is *a friendly*, or their asses are mine."

"So, it's true?" Hanson asked, but not really wanted to.

O'Malley shook his head, "Yes, it was still in the building we raided early this Morning. Nobody yet. They're still sifting through it. Keep me informed?" Hanson nodded. O'Malley looked where the girls were, still with their blankets on the ground and a mess of medical supplies, "Make sure you bag the blankets and watch the damn chain of evidence. That's what we can do for Donovan, to catch this Bitch," he ordered, as Hanson ran his pen through his hair as if saluting.

Poppa Bear and the old Biker raced up to the Roadhouse Grill with the girls, still holding tight, with MacBride's blue Sudan out front. She and Jock came out hearing the bikes. Gina screamed "Mommy!" and grabbed her. Marci got off and ran up to Jock.

Sarah looked at Poppa Bear getting off his bike, holding her hands to her face, shaking her head, and crying with joy. The old Biker joined them, slowly taking his sunglasses off, letting them drop around his neck from a thin black rope, and removed his hat. Duke joined them after arriving in his patrol car, and stared closely at the old Biker. "Malachi!"

All looked with shock. Poppa Bear laughed, and MacBride hugged Malachi. "Thank you for saving my girls, but we lost Donovan."

He looked sharply back at Duke, then Poppa Bear, and they started back for their bikes. "Wait, we need to talk," Duke yelled.

"Later, I will explain it all, later. We need to find Donovan!" They raced off.

MacBride held her girls close. "Daddy dead?" Gina started crying, and she picked her up and took them both with Jock back inside. Duke climbed back into his patrol car and sped off after them with sirens blaring.

The van backed up to the club. Jacquelyn took one of the red bricks from the wall near the door, and removed a key. "This early, no cleaning crew. It should only be Amanda." She opened the door, waved Robin to go first, then followed, picking up a five-foot long metal pipe. They entered the main lobby, and she took the pipe, swung hard, and shattered one of the glass cases. "I always hated these things," and then swung again.

"What the fuck is going on out here!" Amanda yelled as she entered from the fetish pit, in a very tight black body suit, knee-high black boots, and carrying a purple cat-o-nine tail. "Can't have a moment's peace with one of my own bitches!"

Jacquelyn laughed and grabbed the whip from her. "Today, *Ms*. Amanda, you're my bitch!"

She whipped her hard, forcing her to the floor, and she begged her to stop. "No fun when you're on that end, right?"

Robin grabbed the pipe that was in her other hand but started shaking feverishly and collapsed on the floor, before she passed out she saw the device in the same hand alongside the pipe.

"Help, Help!" Amanda cried out.

"You forget, this is a soundproof building and Donovan is not coming to save you. He's dead!" Jacquelyn said, still whipping her hard.

"You lie, whore!" Amanda yelled.

"Sorry, Princess. He was in the building that collapsed early this Morning."

With tears welling up in her eyes, Amanda tries to stand.

"Stay down Bitch!" As she raised the whip again, Amanda dropped back down. Jacquelyn shifted toward the door Amanda had come out of, and looked in, then back at Amanda with a huge smile on her face, and started giggling. "Oh, I am sorry, Madam Mayor. Let me help you out of that," she said, entering the fetish pit. The Mayor screamed as the door closed. The Mayor ran out nude, toward the back rooms. Jacquelyn took Amanda by the hair and pulled her up. "Here!"

She handed her the black diamond studded collar; the Mayor was wearing in the other room. "Put it on!"

Slowly Amanda put the collar on, and she shoved her toward the back door. "Is Sarah here, Bitch?"

"No."

Jackelyn kicked Robin to wake her up and shoved her and Amanda out the back door, against the Van. "Open it," Robin opened it, and she shoved Amanda in. "Home, Bitch."

O'Malley entered the hospital and saw Hanson leaning up against one of the walls. "Report."

He looked through his notepad. "Karen Morgan, the one that spoke at the scene is in the ER, resting. Her sister, Katherine, is in the OR, they're repairing a deep knife wound to her upper right shoulder. Their parents are in the waiting room and Mac and Alice's teams are finishing up with Karen." Hanson reported.

McKnight walked out from the trauma area, in a black three-piece suit. *How can he afford those expensive suits on his salary, he makes less than I do.* O'Malley thought. "Anything?"

He took a toothpick out of his mouth, "Yes, found trace evidence from the ropes, still on their wrist and ankles, did a rape kit on each, should have results soon. They're both scared and resting now, the ER Doctor says, once both are in a room upstairs, we can talk more."

O'Malley ordered and pointed at Hanson. "Find that room, two deputies on the door, a female in the room, and deputies at the nursing station, elevators, and stairs. No one gets in!"

Hanson took off down the way. The girl's parents, her mother with red hair in her late forties, and their Father, a balding dark-haired man in his fifties, came up slowly. The man was holding his wife. "Are you the one who found our girls?" The man asked O'Malley.

"No, Mr. Morgan. All we know at this time is that there is a third girl that was being held with your daughters and was able to help with their release. The deputy you just saw run off, was the first on the scene. He found them walking down Main Street."

The wife let out a cry, and McKnight guided them back to the waiting area. "Let me get you some coffee. This hospital has the best coffee around," he said as he looked back at O'Malley and smiled.

"A third victim was with the serial killer and helping her," Camille leaned over from behind a large high-back chair.

"Not now, please, Camille," O'Malley said, as he moved quickly for the door.

"O'Malley, I am sorry about Donovan, and the other day at the school. You help me, I help you?" Camille yelled running after him.

He stopped at the sliding door, as they kept sliding open and closed in front of him. "Keep Donovan out of the news. No stories till we are completely done," he said, but only looked at the floor.

Biting her lip, "That may be hard. Another station reported his death early this morning."

"Squash it, and I will give you an exclusive when this mess is over," O'Malley said with his eyes closed, knowing he just made a deal with the devil.

"Yes, yes, exclusive. I am all yours," she said cheerfully, dancing around him, shaking him as he rolled his eyes.

Tossing Amanda down into the cellar, "Baby girls, Mommy is home, with a new playmate," Jacquelyn called out, shoving Robin off to the side and closing the doors. "Mommy does not hear her baby girls," she said and turned around. She saw the tables empty, only the jagged file on the table. She screamed and backhanded Robin hard, "You fucking cunt!" Beating her across the face, towards the back wall, and slammed her head into it hard. Robin slouched down on the floor, blood on the wall, while Amanda screamed.

Jacquelyn turned back toward Amanda, "I will finish with her when she wakes up," and shoved Amanda over to the metal tables, taking the jagged knife, cutting her body suit off, blood everywhere, and then went after the boots. Amanda protested and said something about two thousand dollars for them, but Jacquelyn was not listening. She slammed Amanda down onto the table, grabbed more rope, and tied her down. Amanda fought hard, yelled, and she put the red ball gag in her mouth that was lying on the table to shut her up. Looking her body over, running her hands over her body, hard.

"I know it, I know it, you bitch! Rules are only for the staff, you still have your bush, and the drapes do not match the carpet." She laughed loudly, howling as if a madwoman, and snapped. She started running her finger through Amanda's black pubic hair." Amanda screamed and cried.

Jacquelyn heard Robin moaning and moved back towards her. She dragged Robin by her hair and grabbed a pair of scissors, and cut a swatch of her hair off. Then she slammed her on the other table as Amanda looked over with fright, tears still running down her face.

Jacquelyn stripped her remaining clothes off and tied her down, she took a white ball gag from the table and put it in her mouth. She moaned, very groggy from her head wound. Jacquelyn leaned closer to Amanda's ear and said, "I am sorry Ms. Amanda, but there are no safe words here."

Amanda closed her eyes tight, crying more. She pinched her nipples hard and danced around as if drunk, and took a small blade—the bloody knife from—earlier and showed it to her. "Now, let's get started," as she slowly ran the knife blade down and across her belly.

Amanda let out a hellish scream. Jacquelyn giggled and made another cut, causing Amanda to scream again.

History

Even back in 1985, Jackson Hole County was still old-school and backwoods, still deep in the mindset and culture of the late nineteenth century when it came to race and the white man's power. Women and men of color—anyone different from a white male—were nothing; only the white man had power, especially the ones with long, deep roots, running back before the Civil War, and most were for the white man's use and pleasure. Two prominent families dated back the furthest, the Shermans, who ran the town and had whoever they needed or wanted in their back pockets. The other was the Donovans, who always kept an eye on the future, helping others, and could not stand the pain and degradation of the power a white man had, thinking he was superior, and the Shermans, who stood squarely in the past. The families normally avoided each other and stayed clear, except during the Civil War, when it was families versus families.

The Donovan family had stuck to their pride and honor; with the North, the Sherman family paid their way, taking control of their old family money; with the South, fighting for the past, the town became theirs. But they were about to come face to face again, the past slamming into the future. One generation may fall against politics, corruption, and bureaucracy, and one family would not give up, and it could cost them the lives of one, possibly two, generations.

Malachi Donovan raced his sixty-six Corvette, with a single red light on the dashboard, down the old dirt road and slowly pulled up to the lit area with many other patrol cars. Ford Crown Victoria's, brown with a thin single white strip running on each side from the front to just a bit behind the back seat, 'JACKSON HOLE COUNTY, SHERIFF,' along the back fenders. The area was taped off, and the Sherman Estate could be seen off in the distance. A large red tarp laid on the ground, held down in each corner with large rocks because a light wind was kicking up. There were two other Jackson Hole deputies standing nearby, Duke Dubcek, a young deputy with corporal strips and a single star under them. Duke, twenty-five, had red curly hair was and had just promoted to supervisor.

Malachi Donovan, thirty-five, slipping on his black leather jacket over his black jeans and black t-shirt, shield on his waist, seven-point shield gold with blue lettering for JACKSON HOLE COUNTY, on top and LIEUTENANT, curving along the bottom, three-fifty-seven long barrow magnum under his left arm in a shoulder holster, he stepped up to the tarp. Kicking cow shit off his new brown cowboy boots, and holding his new brown cowboy hat, as combed back his brown hair, marine cut, high and tight, with his fingers.

Duke turned seeing him walk up, "Congratulations on the promotion to Lieutenant," as Donovan picked up the tarp by one of the corners and saw the two bodies, two young white girls. It was early morning, and the sun was barely over the horizon, "What you got, Bro!"

Duke rolled his eyes, and took offense with the word, 'Bro,' it did not matter if he was using it as a slang term or just as a link to him, since he recently married Duke's sister, but will never say anything, because he was the closest he will ever have to a Brother. Duke, of Polish descent, most of the town saw him and his sister as second-class citizens since they had only been in Jackson Hole, for two generations, his Grandparents and parents were prisoners in Auschwitz.

"We have two young white girls, eight and eleven, beaten and raped, nude, with no clothing present and no identification. Deputies are still canvassing the area; Coroner is on his way," Duke reported, but Malachi had no expression on his face as he continued looking over the girls.

An oversized white mid-seventies utility van pulls up, 'CORONER' stenciled on the side, an old white man with grey hair, maybe in his late eighties. Black slakes a white dress shirt and suspenders under his oversized white lab coat. A simple backwoods country Doctor moonlighting as the county Coroner, wearing large black-framed Mr. Magoo glasses barely resting on his nose, put out a cigarette, stepped on it, coughed, and lit another, coughed more, and slammed the divers door. "I was planning on going fishing in the morning and starting my Vacation, boys!"

A young, tall Black man in his early twenties, with white slacks, a white dress shirt, and white canvas shoes, wheeled a gurney from behind the van. "No, no Erasmus. Not yet; I haven't looked over the bodies," the old Doctor said as he coughed and spat.

The boy left the gurney and walked up to the old man, "Ol' man, my name is not Erasmus; I keep telling, my name is Richard McKnight," and he followed the old man over to the red tarp.

"This one's bad, Doc," Malachi commented, but the old Doctor just waved him aside.

Raised his glasses and put them on his head, so he could see better. "I have seen it all, boys," he said as he pulled back the red tarp, so all could see. McKnight vomited. Malachi looked at Duke and whispered, Why is he still on the job? and Duke shrugged his shoulders.

"I heard that Lieutenant, how did they ever give you that rank? Damn! And with the old Captain now Sheriff, and who knows before long you might make Captain, boy. Yeah, this is bad, the poor babies," the old Doctor said, scratching his chin.

A young deputy handed some papers and fabrics toward Malachi. "Damn it! Not like this, let me show you again. We have new procedures!" Duke said as he grabbed the deputy by the arm and pulled him away from Malachi, walked him over to his squad car, opened the trunk, placed each item into a separate evident bag, and showed him again how to fill out the paperwork as if teaching him all over again.

Over the next six months, ten more young girls were found near the Sherman Estates, beaten and raped like the first two. The town could not believe how it could happen to their young girls. Every lead Malachi ran down either led him back to the Sherman Estates or a dead end; he knew someone was road-blocking him, pushing him in a different direction each time.

What he heard from the Coroner in describing the rapes was that 'they were not sexual from a man, but objects, some type of wood,' and he could not even accept where the evidence was leading him, involving women and little girls. It was a different time; other places had this but not Jackson Hole; homosexuality was not a topic spoken of openly, and two women and that was against religious law, but it was the first of many dark secrets that were to come out, and he knew the town would never accept it.

All evidence pointed to the Sherman Estates, primarily the Mother and her young Daughter, both suspects in the council's murders, and it started to become an uphill battle to convince the new sheriff and the council of what was truly going on in their sleepily little town. He had heard stories growing up about all the parties most of the women in town had up at Old Lady Sherman's Estate.

Laughed at by many, advised to rethink his conclusions regarding Old Lady Sherman and her Daughter, and even forced out twice, and the new sheriff wanted him to sweep it under the rug. "This does not happen here in Jackson Hole!" he kept telling Malachi. It went on for another six months, and then he finally obtained warrants. A female judge came to the bench, accepted his evidence, and with a handful of deputies including Duke, severed the warrants.

They burst in, and what they found was one of her Saturday night parties, shocked them both. Rumors and in the windows did not do justice to her panties. The women, all between eighteen and fifty, topless or nude, in disturbing sex acts, kissing, licking, and using objects for penetration, and a few beating other women in their sick pleasures. He found chains on the walls in the bedrooms and the basement, with dog dishes, but no little girls. Old Lady Sherman took a shot at Malachi, but when he brought the full evidence and charges, the DA refused to press them, called him mad, and thought he had been drinking.

A week later, he was returning home after continuing the fight for the little girls, when the front window of his sixty-six Corvette was shot out, and he was slammed into a tree and wrapped his classic Corvette around it, killed him, and left his wife, to raise their eleven-year-old Daughter and an eight-year-old Son.

PRESENT DAY

The bullpen was no longer the same. It was no longer loud and busy; it was dead, like Donovan. The bombing hung in the air. No one talked, not even about it, no one was really working, and they all felt the loss of Donovan. He was a friend, a brother, and a nephew. Malachi was alive, and Donovan was dead, the world was upside down.

Duke sat in Donovan's office, holding back the tears and slowly packing up his office. It was the second time he had boxed up the office for a family member. O'Malley slammed his fists down, dropping Malachi's business card, from the first victim and the note from the girl in the park with frustration. He could not take the silence anymore. Everyone turned and looked at him, and Stein had a puzzled look. "God damn it, I will say it. He's dead. We have lost deputies before! I lost a good friend. I am sorry, but we must move on. There is a killer still out there! Business as usual, it's what he would want."

They slowly returned to their own business. Stein walked around his desks. "Anything?"

"The card is a red herring. Donovan told me the other day, she left it for him, another way of playing this fucking mind game with him."

"And the note we found at the park, under the girl?" Stein asked as she picked it up gently by the corners.

"Forensic found the paper matched a piece of notebook paper out of one of the notebooks recovered from the library. It only has one word on it: 'History.'"

Duke took the note, "You think it's a clue directing Donovan to Malachi's old case?"

"Yes, and we need to talk about *his* old case!" O'Malley said, looking at him sternly.

The Mayor ran in barefoot and barely holding onto her black overcoat, tight to her body, and out of breath because she had raced the distance from the club. Not seeing MacBride or Donovan, she looked directly at Stein, remembering her from the club, wiping the tears from her eyes, "She took Ms. Amanda!"

"Ms. Amanda? Who's Ms. Amanda?" O'Malley asked.

"A separate case Donovan and MacBride are working on; I'll talk with the Mayor. This way Madam Mayor, please?" Stein walked the Mayor into the conference room.

"Donovan never left me out of the loop before?" O'Malley said as he watched her enter the conference room.

"A private thing not associated with the killer, and you need to talk with Duke, remember?" Stein said as she followed the Mayor to the conference room.

"Yes," O'Malley answered and looked around, but again Duke had done his disappearing act.

Stein led the Mayor into the conference room, closed the door, and locked it, then closed the blinds, "Jacquelyn took Ms. Amanda?"

Still shaking, "Yes, Ms. Amanda and I were in the fetish pit, she was working me good and hard," still shaking. Stein looked sideways at the Mayor, never hearing of a client, reducing herself to a submissive, "and we heard glass shattering, she went out to check it. I heard voices, and then Jacquelyn came in, untied me, and took my collar, I just ran. Ms. Amanda was on the ground; Mistresses are never on the ground!"

"It's okay, take it slow," Stein said, trying to comfort her, handing her a cup of water from the pitcher on the table. "What happened next?"

"Ms. Amanda was on the floor, like a pet, and Robin was on the ground too, both shaking with a seizure, I think. I was so scared that I just ran, grabbing my keys and coat from my locker. I need to find Sarah," she yelled and turned, grabbing Stein. "She took Ms. Amanda!"

"Jacquelyn has Ms. Amanda?"

A large metal object slammed against a desk in the bullpen, and she could hear a loud male voice yelling. Opening the blinds, saw the Sheriff berating O'Malley. She opened the door.

"Donovan is dead! The case is over. We don't need to re-open old wounds. He failed just like his Father. Close the books, and let it go!" the Sheriff yelled, slamming O'Malley's gun on his desk again.

"Sir, we still have a serial killer out there!" Stein said as he exited the conference room.

"Donovan knew who it was. Go get her, and sweep this mess under the rug."

"Without informing the DA, Sir?" Stein asked.

"I didn't need evidence thirty years ago, and I don't need it now! This is my town," he said, pointing at the Mayor who was now behind

Stein, "my laws," he continued, pointing at O'Malley, "and my damn rules," with his thumb back at himself. "Close it or you're both out of a job!" and stormed out.

O'Malley's frustration built, and he shoved everything off his desk, even his own gun that the Sheriff slammed down, and watched his wife's picture fall onto the floor.

Construction workers were slowly cleaning the blast site, moving rubble and glass to dumpsters. The whole North Mammoth motorcycle club rode up, with over thirty men, revving their bikes. The workers darted off in all directions as they saw this massive group surrounding them like an invading army. O'Malley followed with lights and sirens; he and Duke joined them.

"Where was my Son when the blast went off?" Malachi demanded of O'Malley as he slammed him up against his SUV.

O'Malley looked at him closely and sharply. Knowing all the reports and history, he claimed he was dead. He looked at Duke as he came around the SUV. Duke saw the look on O'Malley's face and Malachi's, always knowing that this day would come. The past finally caught up with him, and the town.

Angus stepped from behind Malachi and stood between them. "Help us, brother? We may not have much time."

He guided them over the rubble to where the entrance was. All followed, climbing over the debris: glass, rebar, and concrete, toward the area where the computer room was, three stories above them. But now, it was just the rubble around them, where Donovan was before the blast. "I was there, he was here, inside the room," he said as he pointed back a bit from where he was standing. "He entered the room, then two SWAT members, and I heard him yell for them to get out."

"When we were in Fallujah in the last days, Donovan and I were caught in a blast and buried for two days. Our team found us both under the rubble inside a dome. The last thing Donovan said to me was, 'the sheik's gambit,' his plan before we left told me there was a dome here. Dig!" Angus explained and yelled.

All including Duke and O'Malley helped move the rubble away, they tossed it everywhere, finding a thick steel dome, five feet around, and a few feet under the rubble. They dug down fast, unearthing a still encased dome. It sat about four feet high. O'Malley looked at the dome, then at his Brother. "There is no way he could have survived under that. It's been almost eight hours!"

Malachi grabbed O'Malley by his collar again and pointed at the three holes on top. "My Son is a Damn Navy Seal! He can hold his breath, and there are three air holes." Then he squatted down and yelled into one of the holes, "Sonny!" But they hear nothing. He pounded on the dome with his fists through his grief, then picked a long thick pipe, about three feet long, bashed on the dome hard, and waited.

Duke heard three soft taps. "You hear that?"

Malachi banged again, harder. He held the pipe with both hands and slammed it down. They heard three muffled taps, and he looked back at Angus. Angus snapped his fingers. "Frankenstein!"

Frankenstein pushed himself through the crowd, stooped down, reached under the dome, and with all his strength, tossed it over and away, as if it were made of tissue paper, and revealed Donovan, he was lying on his side in a hole about three feet down, holding a pipe and gasping for air. His upper tactical chest gear was removed.

Malachi and Duke jumped into the hole. "I got you, Sonny. I got you," Malachi yelled and pulled him up on his legs. Donovan coughed, looked up at the old Biker with the old, weary gray goatee, and heard 'Sonny,' and it harkened back to a time when he was a boy, about to hit a beehive with a stick, and heard his Dad call out, "You disturb that hive, Sonny, with that stick. I will tan your bottom so hard that you will not be able to sit for a month. You hear me, Sonny."

"Do you hear me Sonny? I got you!" Malachi said.

Angus called out for water. Donovan looked closer at the old Biker, who was looking down at him, and through the old gray hair and goatee, "Dad?" with a weakened and hoarse voice as the old Biker held him closer, "Yes, Sonny, it's me. I got you."

The crowd let out a loud cheer, and Duke slapped Malachi on his shoulder. Then, the Donovan family rejoiced.

MacBride and Stein ran frantically down the hospital corridor, deputies everywhere. Through a curtain, Hanson was standing next to and holding open as they ran through. They stopped and MacBride let out a gasp. Donovan was hooked up to monitors, with an air mask on his mouth and nose. He pulled the mask from his face, "Trust me …" he said with a hoarse voice, she sat on the side of his bed, grabbed him, and kissed him, a long deep kiss.

Stein moved toward O'Malley who was off to one side, and asked, "Where did you find him?"

"Angus and his Dad did, under a huge dome at the bottom of the blast site," O'Malley informed them.

With shock, she looked back at them, and then with a questioning look about his Dad, toward O'Malley and, he waved her off, a story for another time, "How did Angus know?"

"You got me," he said. They were in one during their last days in Fallujah and trapped for days."

Donovan kissed MacBride back fondly, and then turned toward O'Malley. "The Sheik's gambit," Donovan whispered. "I had an idea. The building would be rigged to blow and saw a dome on the roof as we drove in off the ramp, it reminded me of my last mission in Fallujah. I told Angus, in case I was right and couldn't get out in time, I would be under that, and he would try for the girls, as our team did for us as we cleared the building," Donovan explained.

MacBride hit him hard. "Why didn't you tell me!"

"If I was right about the bomb, I would only have enough time to send a quick message. Only Angus would have understood."

"We have more problems, T. Since the report of your death, history is coming back to haunt us all. The sheriff has told me to sweep it under the rug," O'Malley explained.

"And she has Ms. Amanda and Robin," Stein added.

MacBride looked at Stein with shock, and then back at Donovan, and under his breath replies, "Fuck!"

"Who is Ms. Amanda?" O'Malley demanded.

"A personal issue," Donovan said as he started taking the IVs and monitor cables off, "Keep the report of my death, we need to talk to Duke and my Dad."

"What are you doing?" MacBride asked, as he pushed off the bed and moved around. "You can't leave."

"I can't sit here and let them win," Donovan said.

"It's too late for your death unless my friend the devil can squash it," O'Malley said.

Donovan knew Camille was the devil O'Malley spoke of. "Call her. We will need her help. My death may buy us some time," Donovan said and all looked confused.

"I am here with Detective Ferguson O'Malley, Lieutenant Donovan's late partner. Can you tell us what you found after searching the blast site?" Camille asked.

Doing the best acting job he could, O'Malley replied, "Yes, Camille. After a thorough search of the blast site and surrounding area, we did find Lieutenant Donovan's body. He had been…" he said, as the camera turned slowly watching two paramedics walk past Camille with a body bag.

Donovan stood with a sling around his left arm, turned off the television, and tossed the remote on the bar. "This should buy us some time."

Malachi, Duke, and O'Malley sat at four smaller tables that had been pushed together, boxes sitting on top. Stein was at the bar with MacBride, near him. He looked at his Dad, who walked up. They hugged and held each other for a moment. Malachi slapped his Son. "I am sorry Sonny, it was for the best, back then."

"I am starting to understand, Pops. It's very good to have you back. I wish Annabelle lived to see it," Donovan said slapping his shoulder.

With a few tears in their eyes, "Yes, but now let's bring you all up to speed." Donovan said and the ladies joined the others at the table.

"Duke and I were stonewalled thirty years ago. It could have been the Middle Ages here, and the town would not accept the sex acts up at the Sherman Estates as is so common today, with the Pearl Drop Club, except for the death of the little girls," Malachi explained, as he looked at the group, then the ladies, and finally Donovan, with a pleasing look on his face, with acceptance for what Annabelle had created.

MacBride looked at Donovan and remembered their little excursion out at the Sherman Estate and all he told her, "So Jacquelyn wanted to stop Old Lady Sherman?"

"Yes, for years of cruelty she and her Mother did to her, and she does not believe what she is doing is wrong, like most Psychopaths and Pedophiles, but yes. She couldn't take what happened to her when she was younger and with the younger girls, and her Grandmother's constant abuse."

"I understand that and same-sex relationships, but why the little girls? I never got a chance to figure that out," Malachi asked.

"What I have read in your old case files, and still waiting on the missing reports," Donovan said as he looked sharply at Duke, "You were close, some Psychopaths are Pedophiles, tending to the young ones, and for some reason, Old Lady Sherman prefers them before puberty and girls. I learned that Captain Grant was also an incestuous child of old man Sherman and their Daughter."

All looked with disbelief. "He was disowned at eleven, after being used like Jacqueline and the other girls. That is why we never found his background."

"How?" Stein asked.

"Mac found his DNA match with the Shermans," Donovan answered.

"DNA was so new back then and could have been a big help," Duke said, "compared to today."

McKnight walked in with a few files, "Why was I not invited to this…" he started and then saw Malachi. "Boss, is that you?" His elegant style and voice turned back into that young Black boy for a moment, how most whites had preferred him back then.

Malachi stood, shook his hand. "Richard here, as a big help back then, was just a young kid who helped the coroner," McKnight rolled his eyes remembering that old bastard. "But one hell of a forensic tech, and learned very fast."

"I learned everything from you, Boss." McKnight said smiling, then stood up straighter, "Good to have your Dad back, right, T?"

Donovan stood and took McKnight's hand, "Yes, you will join us, once I get the last warrants."

McKnight nodded, "From what Duke has been telling me, about the Sheriff, I will join him when he arrests the Sheriff. I want to see the look on that old Bastard's face when I walk into his office." Malachi said.

"Good, have you found Mrs. Davendish?" Donavan asked looking at both Stein and MacBride.

"Yes, she is in one of the cells waiting, I was going to interview her, in the morning, but now that you're back, you can enjoy the fun, " Stein replied.

"We will interview her together, not leaving you out of any fun with that case," Donovan smiled.

"So, what's your plan, Sonny?" Malachi asked.

"After I talk with Mrs. Davendish about a second case, I will talk to Judge Wilkinson about the warrants ----"

"She's still on the bench. She was my only help back then," Malachi cut him off.

Donovan nodded. "Yes, then at the same time, we will raid the Sherman Estate. Well, you, Duke, and Hanson arrest the Sheriff.

"Let's get to work," Donovan said as Malachi slapped his shoulder again, and he winced.

Jock brought over two bottles of Scotch, and a few glasses, and placed them on the table, "Good, but we still can't ignore the elephant in the room. Hell, you're alive?"

Malachi poured a glass, took a quick drink, and looked at Duke. "With some help from Duke, too."

Donovan looked sharply at Duke again; he knew Duke never told him the whole story of his father's death.

Malachi handed the bottle back to Jock, who poured drinks for the rest of them, "I hit the tree, and whoever was shooting at me blasted out the window."

"Took me ten years and over fifty thousand dollars to rebuild it," Donovan commented. "It sat there for over eight years.

"And almost took someone here, two seconds to destroy it," Malachi commented as he winked at MacBride, who smiled back. All remembering how she nearly crashed it into one of the armored trucks, but knowing she was distraught over her girls.

"I don't know how long I laid there, had to be hours, bleeding and maybe with a concussion. Somehow, Duke found me," Donovan shot another look at Duke with anger. "He wanted to take me to the hospital, but I refused." Donovan's anger subsided. "I told him to take me to Miko." Malachi explained.

Stein looked at Donovan, the only one who did not know her, "Who?"

"Mai's Mother, you know, the woman at the bar, the other day," Donovan answered.

"She fixed me up. I don't know how long I was out. When I was better, Duke told me the Sheriff closed it all and told everyone who ever speaks of it again, would not be living long. I know I could not return then for your Mother's and Annabelle's sake," Malachi explained.

"The roses! That was you, who left them on Mom's and Annabelle's graves each year?" Donovan remembered.

"Yes, every year on their birthdays."

"But why the Knights?" O'Malley asked, "I think my Brother would have told me."

"Club rules, copper," Malachi said and laughed. "My old friend Butch from the Corp, the leader of the Knights then, and Miko's husband, said it would be for the best to hide out. No one would look for me in their ranks. I have been watching the Sheriff ever since. I was glad when I heard the case was hot again, and seeing you walk into the bar, I was proud of you with how you handled yourself."

"He was just a hang around, didn't know what I was going to do with the other twenty or so," Donovan said, giggling.

"Malachi laughed. "Sonny, you're a fucking Navy Seal, I knew you could have handled yourself, especially with the Master Sergeant on your six," he said as he saluted Stein, who smiled. "I know she had your back, Navy."

"Thank you, Sergeant Major," Stein replied.

Donovan looked at the label on the whiskey, then at Jock. "This is from my private stock. You got two bottles of the thirty-year-old Scotch."

"Ah, *my* private reserve. Remember, you won the bar in the poker game. You still owe me for the reserve, and it's a celebration. Your Dad is alive," Jock said as MacBride smacked Donovan on his left shoulder. He winced again. Jock smiled and shook Malachi's hand. The room exploded in laughter as Malachi poured Donovan another glass.

Last Pieces

Donovan was back in his office, and the station was back to normal as Duke laid two large file boxes on Donovan's desk. "Last six months of missing preteen girls, and preteen Jane Does."

"Have Scott match them with the dead girls that were reported over the last three years?"

Duke took the boxes back out and placed them on the long table in the bullpen, where Hanson was sitting. O'Malley entered, "Mrs. Davendish is in interrogation and the Mayor is in the conference room." Donovan moved back toward his office. O'Malley stopped him placed a hand on his chest, and said, "Why am I out of the loop with this part of the case?"

Donovan closed the door. "I am sorry, Ferg. I did plan to tell you the links before Amanda's disappearance, my late Sister's partner at the Pearl Drop Club. She had told me a few things that were going on there, and asked me to look into it, which Sarah and I did. At first, there was no link, but then we found Jacquelyn worked there. . ."

"Annabelle owned the club?" O'Malley cut him off.

Donovan looked around, making sure no one was listening. "Ferg, don't let that out. I own the Pearl Drop Club now." O'Malley's eyes widened, and with a smile, he said, "Keep that under your hat!"

Giggling, "Yes, I will."

"Promise me!"

He nodded, and Stein knocked on the door. "She's waiting?"

"I should be in there," O'Malley said.

"Trust me, it's nothing that concerns you. She is not associated with the Sherman case," Donovan said.

Donovan and Stein entered the interrogation room where Mrs. Davendish was waiting, sitting behind the table, cuffed to the ring. She was not pleased with how she had been treated this way, like a common criminal. The blinds were lowered over the two-way mirror and Donovan closed and locked the door. "What the hell do you think you're doing, Mr. Donovan? Your Sister would turn over in her grave if she knew a male was looking into the happenings inside the Pearl Drop Club!"

Donovan and Stein sat, and he placed two folders on the table, taking out a photo of each of the girls from the hospital, each with bruises and cuts on their faces. Mrs. Davendish looked them over, with no emotion or remorse. Donovan waited, and she finally spoke, "What happens at the Pearl. . ."

Donovan slammed the table, and Stein jumped, but Mrs. Davendish just sat there, "Not when you put two girls in the hospital and rape them!"

She said nothing, and he pulled the medical report out, and read, "Patient, presented with multiple bruising on face, chest, and legs, with a Midline Facture along her frontal lobe, and vaginal and anal tearing, and bruising due to a foreign object or objects. You broke her skull and raped her, for what, and why in the basement?"

"I would like to call my Lawyer now, Lieutenant Donovan?" Mrs. Davendish said coldly.

Donovan laughed, again slammed the table, and looked at Stein, who was smiling. "You accuse me of having my Sister turning over in her grave because a male is looking into the Pearl Drop Club. Where, we both know, what happens inside, staying inside, and you ask for a Lawyer, knowing all too well, there is no way in hell, my Sister would allow rape! If she were alive, she would beat the hell out of you, and still serve the time."

Mrs. Davendish rubbed the side of her mouth, fixing her lipstick, knowing that it was over but hoping not to show it, and shifted in her chair. "Can we make a deal?"

"I have to report the beatings and rapes and arrest you for that. So, you will have those charges." Donovan explained.

"Can you leave the Pearl Drop Club out of it?" she said with a coy look, trying to be a little miss innocent in her red strapless dress.

"I am not sure yet how to leave it out. If I can legally, you will confess to the charges, serve the jail time, pay restitutions, and never return to the club," Donovan explained looking directly at her.

She thought it over. "Yes." Stein quickly spun a legal yellow pad around, which had been sitting in front of her, slid it over to her, and placed a pen on top.

"I want it all, detail for detail, and word for word. I want everything that you did to them both, there, and I mean everything!" Donovan said, still with his glare shooing right at her.

Mrs. Davendish looked directly back at him. "But you know I can't talk about the club."

"This you can. I will be the only one reading it, so do not leave a damn thing out. Think of it as you used to tell my sister about a special pet you wanted. That much detail."

Her face turned beet red. "Well, I never!"

Stein giggled.

Donovan smiled and tapped the legal pad. "Leave nothing out."

"I do this for Annabelle, not you."

Donovan got up, and Mrs. Devenish raised her hands in the cuffs as if to tell him she could not write with these on. "Detective Stein will undo your cuffs once I leave. She will stay in the room till you're done, and then return you to a cage, and give me the story for my eyes only," Donovan said, looking down at Stein. After the word 'cage,' Stein nodded in agreement. "After I read it, then I will decide where we can go from there."

The Mayor was pacing back and forth in the conference room, smoking to calm her nerves. The blinds were closed, and Donovan entered. She ran up to him as he kicked the door closed and quickly pushed a small circular disk holding paper clips across the table. She saw it and put her cigarette out, then hugged him. "Camille reported, you were dead!"

"Part of my plan to keep the Sheriff, Jacquelyn, and the Shermans blind, and to show the case was closed, per the Sheriff," Donovan explained as he pulled back from her embrace.

"Yes, Jacquelyn has Ms. Amanda and Robin. What are *we* going to do?" the Mayor asked, trying to hug him again, but he sat her down."

"Well, the department must keep up the charade that O'Malley has closed the case, and I'm dead. I have the Knights watching for Jacquelyn and out at the Sherman Estate."

"The Knights, they're a bad group. They won't help you."

He took a seat across from her. "You may not remember when my Father died."

"Yes, I remember my parents talking about his death after it happened."

"He did not die and has been in hiding, since."

She looked at him with confusion. "What?"

"No time to explain. What I need you to do is do what you normally do: be the Mayor, keep my death out there. If anyone asks, we need business as usual, and I know you can do that, Catherine."

"But Ms. Amanda . . ."

"Your normal life does not involve the club, right?" Donovan asked coldly. She nodded. "You will be okay, and I know you can do this, Catherine. Do it for Annabelle."

She nodded again, wiping tears off her face. There was a knock at the door; Donovan looked through the blinds. It was Stein, and he opened the door. "That was fast?"

"I have Deputy Scott with her. She is still writing and asked for a second pad. You have … guests in your office. They asked me to find you," Stein said. He let her in, making sure no one saw him behind the door and no one other than who needed to know he was alive.

"Will you please take the Mayor home and meet me at the back door of the club in two hours," Donovan asked as he checked at his watch. "And bring a few female deputies?"

Stein nodded, looked down at the Mayor, as Donovan hurried to his office, and closed the door. The blinds were closed, Malachi was sitting behind his desk, and Angus was on the couch, with both of his legs up on the coffee table.

He swung around in the chair. "Same old office, same desk, but what a great chair. All I had was one of those old wooden straight-back ones."

Donovan looked at Angus, and then back at his Dad in his chair, and he felt like a kid on Christmas morning. "I believe you're here because you have something?"

Both laughed. Malachi laid twenty on the desk and looked at Angus. "He was never a fun kid." both winked at each other as Angus took the twenty, seemingly winning some bet, Donovan thought.

"I was fun, you just were never around, after I turned eight," Donovan blurted out before thinking.

Malachi looked at him, a bit stern, and then laughed again. "See, I told you, he can't even take a joke." Then Malachi snapped his fingers for the twenty back, but Angus put it in his inside pocket.

Donovan shook his head and then looked at Angus. "What?"

Angus stood up. "We followed the Daughter and a nurse around for the last two days. This morning, they picked up some food and beverages for a party and grabbed four girls, and hurried back to the house. Possibly something up this weekend?"

"I don't know what they told them, but the girls got right into the car," Malachi added.

"Where did they pick the girls up, and did you get pictures?" Donovan said as he looked at both men.

"I was a detective once, Sonny. I remember how this is done, and they were near their school," he answered and slapped his chest with an old evidence bag from thirty years ago, with four Black media cards. "I hear you can get these back within minutes, unlike days, back then."

Donovan picked up his desk phone. "Get in here!"

There was a knock at the door; he looked through the blinds. Duke came in. "Is everything going as planned?" Donovan asked.

"Yes, O'Malley is across town working with the Sheriff on a bank robbery case, hoping the Sheriff is thinking he is off this one," Duke explained.

Holding the bag out to him, "Get this fast!"

Duke took the bag and saw it was an old one from way back when and looked at Malachi. Donovan opened the door for him to leave, "Any sign of Jacquelyn?"

"Nope, and we have been watching the Estate and Club, one crew did see the Van for a time around town, but lost it," Angus replied.

"We need eyes on her," Donovan said and picked up the phone again, "Now."

Hanson knocked on the door and entered with cuffs, Angus saw them and assumed the position with hands behind his back and he walked them out, with two other deputies waiting outside the door and continued escorting them out the front, placing them into a patrol car. Hanson looked at Malachi in the back seat, and he winked back, and the patrol car drove off. If anyone questioned, it was just a couple of bikers being hassled, which most in town would accept.

The judge's office was grand, with two walls of bookshelves with law books: one behind her desk, and the other off to her left. An American flag was in the right corner behind the desk. The oversized desk was cluttered with files and law books and rested atop a desk calendar. Malachi and Donovan sat waiting. Malachi leaned back with his boots up on the desk, Judge Samantha Wilkinson, entered, black hair with some graying in a long judicial robe, sat, and looked at Malachi, "Donovan, I would have come to your office to discuss this case to keep your death a secret, and I have told you about bring *your* felons or riffraff into my office, before." Wilkinson said not realizing or placing the old biker.

Both men looked at each other and laughed, Donovan slapped Malachi's legs, and Malachi took his boots off her desk, "I think, you need to take a closer look at *my* riffraff, Samantha. You may be surprised?"

She looked quickly at Donovan and then took a hard look at the old Biker with his old cowboy hat, she moved around her desk, for a better look at his boots, and Malachi stood, and placed his hat on his chest, "Malachi . . . you ol' son of a bitch!" she hugged him.

"Yes, it's me, Sam,"

"But you're dead! I went to your funeral."

He sat back down as she moved back around her desk, "Yes, and thank you for that, with all the politics back then, it was better for all parties, that I stayed dead."

She nodded, Donovan handed her five warrants, and she placed them in front of herself, and leaned back, crossed her arms, "I am going to tell you what I told him, thirty years ago, when he came to me with this, too. Watch your step and be damn careful. I will add, most of this town still has not grown up, hell, most are still in the nineteenth century, or the Middle Ages, and will never consider the twentieth nor twenty-first. It has taken me these thirty years to get to where I am, and I do hope you don't take me down with you both, you hear me, old man." She said, then looked over at Malachi and then back down over the warrants, she stopped, laid the others down but kept one in her hand, and looked showed one to them, and then right at Donovan, "If this one works, I reiterate, I hope I am not brought down with you two."

"Yes, I thought that one might get your attention," Donovan said.

She signed the first four, read over the last one carefully again, for the Sheriff, and then signed it, "Good luck, boys."

Donovan took them all, looked through them, and handed the one for the Sheriff to Malachi, "I do believe this one is yours, Pops. I hope you enjoy bringing down your old friend."

Wilkinson smiled and watched as Donovan left. "He is no buddy of mine, Sonny. But I will enjoy bringing that old bastard down, once and for all.

"Donovan?" Wilkinson said and he turned back toward her, "I do thank you, for leaving the Club out of all of this . . . Annabelle would be pleased," Wilkinson said, and Malachi smiled in agreement.

"Yes, Ma'am," Donovan said.

The sixty-six Corvette pulled up to the backdoor of the Club, Stein waited with four other female deputies. Donovan pulled a brick from the wall, but the key was no longer there. He looked back at Stein and pulled one out of his wallet, "Was only to be used in an Emergency. . ."

Deputy Scott, Hanson's partner stepped up, and she placed her hand over his hand with the key, "I know Annabelle would understand," said as the other deputies and Stein looked down for a moment with respect.

Roberts opened the door; Donovan looked up at her, "You think you're the only one with a key," She told him holding one up with her hand and a smile, as Stein looked down slowly.

Donovan put his key away and advised them all, "We'll talk about that later," he was not happy she had one.

Roberts smiled and turned around and they followed her in, "I have been working for about an hour and have found a few things," Roberts explained as Donovan, Stein, and the deputies joined her in the main lobby. Donovan saw two other techs working, one from Robert's team and the brunette, he saw that handed McKnight the paper in the Museum with the DNA results, both in blue jumpsuits. There was tape around both smashed cases, and a ruler card around the pipe that Jacquelyn left, with an additional one next to it. He could also see a few evidence bags on the counter.

"An hour?" Donovan questioned her, as he looked at his watch, "More like you all have been, here all morning."

She checked her watch, "Oops, I mean six, we came at closing, five am." Roberts reported, with a grin.

"Shall we, Alice," Donovan said with his hands out as if to ask her to dance.

"I read the report Stein took down from the Mayor and what we found and what we have found here. Stein, will you play Robin, I will play Jacquelyn. Scott?" Roberts said wavering at Scott, "You and

Margot will play the Mayor and Ms. Amanda. Please step in the room for now," She pointed to Scott and one of the techs, the brunette, and they exited into the fetish pit, as the other tech and deputies joined Donovan on the opposite side of the room near the entrance to the Ballroom. Roberts picked up the pipe with her gloved right hand, and walked back into the hallway with Stein, "Ready?"

"Impress me," Donovan said.

She and Stein came in quickly; she swung the pipe at one of the shattered cases, and then the other. "From the report I read, Ms. Amanda came out after hearing the glass shattering, Scott, you can come out now," She yelled, and Scott joined them, "Mad at seeing this and mad that she was being interrupted. As The Mayor said she heard someone being whipped hard," Roberts explained and motioned Scott over toward her and down onto the floor, she knelt. Roberts picked up the larger bag with the whip from the counter, "Whipping her down, she then moved over to the door," and opened it. "She went in for some time. Then the Mayor said, she untied her and took her collar, and told her to leave. She ran out."

She then motioned to the tech in the room, she ran out and behind Donovan, "She came out, and whipped Ms. Amanda more, the Mayor heard. Then saw as she peeked out of the ballroom. Robin was on the floor holding the bar, shaking and she moved back into the ballroom until they left, still listening. She shoved them out the back and had Ms. Amanda put her collar on. We found chalk here, here, and at the back door." Pointing first, at each case, then the fetish pit door, and finally down the hallway. "We also found this on the floor next to the pipe," Roberts explained as she picked up another smaller bag off the counter, and handed it to Donovan "I think it's her garage door opener?"

Donovan looked it over, held it gently on the corner, not to taint the evidence, gave it back, and walked behind the counter, waved Roberts, Stein, and Scott, to follow, he started rummaging for something, under the counter, "Stein, you're new to the club, Scott, I am not sure what you enjoy here, and knowing my Sister, I have an idea. And Alice, we'll talk about your time here, since you have a key,

later." Donovan said to each of them, Scott smiled at him, and he found a small cardboard box, tossed it on the counter, and put his hand out, Roberts handed him a glove, "As clients, I do believe you remember these?"

"Never used them, what are they?" Roberts asked.

"They are control devices for pets. They work with collars," Donovan said as he pulled two out, two silver large collars, with a small red bulb on each, and took the bag back from Alice, looked at it on one side, "This one is cranked up full. It was why the Mayor thought Robin was having a seizure, and got them for here. Very good dance, you did with the crime scene," Donovan complimented Roberts, and she winked.

"So where are Ms. Amanda and Robin?" Stein asked.

"That I don't know, the knights have not seen her Van in some time, and not at the Sherman Estate. But I am here to see the basement." Donovan said all looked back at him with confusion never heard of that room before.

"The two girls, Mrs. Davendish had taken down there, beaten and abused. Amanda said no one goes into the basement," Donovan explained, and each looked at him with confusion, since he did not use the title, 'Ms.'

"Where is the basement?" Stein asked.

"Over here," he said, as he led them through the ballroom, to the back, and through the double doors into the private rooms. He walked through and they hesitate, "Do I have to take each one of you over my damn knee for my sister's sake, are you coming?" Donovan yelled back, each knew unless they were in play, they would not enter the private rooms, "are you clients, are professionals, now!"

Stein pushed the swinging doors open, and they followed.

Donovan looked over the four black doors, set in the white walls, each with a doorframe, and saw the door he crashed through the other day was fixed, "Here," he said as he pointed at the one door without a doorframe, to his left. He turned the knob but found it locked. He kicked it open and heard metal hitting the ground, downstairs, he grabbed his navy SIG and ran down the stairs, Stein, and Scott followed with their guns drawn. As they reached the bottom they saw, Rachel, the other girl who screened the front door with Robin, she was naked, and tied to the center pole, "She went that way!" Rachel yelled and pointed with her head toward a dark corner in the back of the room, and they heard a huge steel plate slam down onto the floor.

"Got her?" Donovan called out to Scott, as she stooped down near Rachel, while he and Stein headed off into the back, into a corner, behind a metal shelve unit, only to find the corner of the room. Donovan pulled out a small pocket flashlight, and scanned the corner, only to find an old steel sewer cap, a manhole cover, and a crowbar, near it. He took the crowbar with his right hand, still with the glove. Opened the manhole cover and looked in with the flashlight, "Tell O'Malley to place squad cars, at each of the manhole covers in a three-mile radius, I don't think she can run far," He ordered, then jumped into the hole, and slammed the manhole cover down over him.

Stein stepped back as it hit the floor. She moved out of the corner and saw Roberts and a tech placing a blanket around Rachel.

"O'Malley, you there?" Stein said after she pulled her radio out of her back pocket.

"Yea," O'Malley said over the radio.

"Station deputies at all manhole covers, in a three-mile radius of the club, she is on the run."

"What!"

"His orders!"

"Check," O'Malley answered with disgust, she could tell in his voice that he was still not happy, being left out.

She watched as Scott and the techs took Rachel out, "So, let's see what this room has to offer, and why Ms. Amanda wanted no one down here."

The room was large, with many boxes, and some bloodstains on the floor, other than that, nothing. Stein then saw something on the far wall underneath the staircase and ran her hand up and down the wall following a seam. Stepped back, and turned her flashlight, but Roberts pulled a cord hanging above them and turned the light on under the stairs. They could see the wall better; Stein pushed the corner of the wall at the far end under the stairs, away from the seam, and it swung open.

They moved back around and were in awe at what they saw in the new room.

Donovan shoved the heavy manhole cover up with his shoulder, a gun drawn. Duke and Hanson were there, Duke nodded to Hanson to show it was good, and Hanson pulled the manhole cover back, Duke offered his hand, and helped him out, winded from running, "Report!"

"No sign of her yet, but some of the knights found the Van dumped in a deserted alley off Pine, McKnight and his teams are en route."

"How far?"

"Two miles from the club," Duke answered, as Hanson handed Donovan a bottle of water.

"She should have come out near here; I went down three access tunnels, and they were dead ends."

O'Malley pulled up, "What's going on?"

"We found Rachel, the other door girl, who worked with Robin, in the basement of the club, and after hearing a manhole cover closing, I went after her. I will have to wait for Stein's report." Donovan said, drinking and catching his breath. O'Malley looked at him, still not pleased with being left out. "I am sorry, Ferg. I need to respect my Sister's wishes. What happens at the Pearl Drop club, stays at the Pearl Drop club," Duke held his tears back, O'Malley understood, but was still pissed.

Angus and Malachi rode up, "You heard about the Van?" Malachi asked.

"Yes, thanks. So, you and Duke heading out?" Donovan asked as he looked at Malachi and then Angus.

"Out?" O'Malley asked.

"When Stein and I raid the Sherman Estate, Duke and Malachi will arrest the Sherriff. You and Hanson will hold the outside," Donovan explained.

O'Malley turned red, steaming mad. After all this, he could go to the party, but not step on the dance floor. He pointed at Donovan and flipped his hand back to a thumb, to have him follow him and they climbed into the SUV. Angus and Malachi rode off, Hanson started taping off the scene, and   Duke returned to his patrol car and tried to compose himself. Hanson blocked the other side of the road.

"I respect you and love you like a brother, hell if it wasn't for you, my Brother would be dead, but there is no way in hell you are keeping me from

this party and not being allowed inside, T!" O'Malley demanded.

"I am not keeping from the party but for the respect of some of the women in town, it will be me, Stein, and all the female deputies, she can find, who will crash the party. You will control the perimeter, I am sorry, but it has to be this way." Donovan advised.

"I would rather take down the Sheriff, personally. After how he berated me when we thought you were dead. And how he abused Sarah and the girls, with

"Good, then coordinate with Duke."

Stein walked into Donovan's office as he was skimming a report, "We cleared the basement?"

"Sorry," Donovan said as an afterthought, and looked up, "how is Rachel?"

"She's good, a little bit scared more than anything, Jacquelyn had just stripped her, hadn't even started when you kicked in the door."

"What about the basement?"

"Nothing but some boxes, old blood stains, but the hidden room . .

He cut her off sharply. "It's not relative to the cases!"

"No, but you . . . "

"No, I don't, you don't either, never talk about that room, and tell Alice and whoever else was with you, to forget it!" Donovan orders.

She looks at him, questioning. During her short period with him. She has never seen him go off on anyone. *Did I hit a nerve?* Stein thought.

"Never talk about that room!"

Endgame

Dana and Alice sat outside a café, alone on Main Street, having coffee, enjoying their afternoon, and flirting, Alice ran her foot up Dana's leg, and Dana caressed her hand, they looked around casually making sure no one saw them. Dana wore a skimpy white flowery sundress, unlike her normal black business suits, Alice was in a black running suit, a young blonde waitress, was wearing a white dress skirt, black leggings, black ankle-high boots, and a black dress shirt, and name tag said 'Maggie,' and a green apron, and she laid down the check on the table, near Alice, smiled toward both of them. Both were still watching to make sure no one could see them and enjoying each other's time that they did not see Donovan pulled up a chair and sat down quickly.

He lowered his voice so others could not hear him, "Ladies, I am sorry to disturb you, but I have been looking for you both for a special assignment."

Both locked eyes and then back at him, "The Pearl Drop Club?" Roberts asked.

"Yes, but also something major," he looked around, "I want you both to find as many female deputies as possible on your teams, for the raids on the club and then the Sherman Estate. I don't wish to have any males, enter either site, other than me and my dad, if he arrives in time, so I can respect Annabelle, and keep it quiet for the town, and up at the Sherman Estate, for the little girls, if any are there."

Both thought about it for a moment, then nodded, "How many will you need, you think?" Stein asked.

"Nine for the club, and say . . . fifteen for the Sherman Estates," Donovan said.

"What about O'Malley? I have started to feel he does not wish to be left out of anything, since I started," Stein said.

"True, I told him my plan for only females, and he did blow his stack," Donovan started, Stein laughed, understanding what he meant, "but once the Sheriff slammed him in front of the department, he jumped at helping my dad and Duke taking the Sheriff down."

"Your father. . . Roberts asked.

"Long story, you both in?"

"Yes," answered together.

"OK, find the teams, and meet me back at the Roadhouse Grill tomorrow at noon. Sorry to spoil your day off and your night, I know you have special plans," Donovan said, winked, smiled, and walked off, taking the check with him, each smile back.

"I have all the warrants, you up for it?" Donovan asked.

Sarah raised her head slowly, holding Marci, next to her, and Gina in her lap, "I'll be there, let me know when?" she whispered with tears in her eyes still, but he could see the rage she had for the Sheriff for taking her girls.

Donovan kissed her on the head, then Marci, and finally Gina, and then looked back at them as he opened the door, she smiled.

Jock was outside the bar near Donovan's red fifties classic pickup truck, cleaning and loading shotguns, and two rifles, as Donovan pulled up in the sixty-six, followed by Duke, in his patrol car, O'Malley in his SUV, Donovan climbed out, shook

each man's hand. They all turned back and heard Malachi and Angus riding up, Malachi climbed off his oversized Indian bike and pulled a sawed-off twelve-gauge shotgun, from his saddlebags, and tossed it to Jock, who started cleaning it, and then loaded it.

"We're ready, Sonny?" Malachi asked as he saw the concern on Donovan's face.

"In a minute, Pops," Donovan said slapping Jock on the shoulder and climbing into his trailer.

O'Malley pulled a small silver flask out, and took a swig, "You're on the job, Brother," Angus advised him, and he wiped his lips and put it away.

Donovan picked up a picture of his mother and Annabelle, back in the eighties, Annabelle was about fifteen, with long red hair, and his mother with reddish brown hair, you could see it darkening and thinning from the chemo. There were dirty clothes tossed around the room as well as pizza boxes and beer bottles. He gave up after the divorce, "This one is for you, Annabelle. Both the Sherriff and Jacquelyn have disrespected you," He kissed the picture, and walked out, and handed the picture to Malachi, "here." Malachi took it, looked at it, smiled, and then nodded.

"Be careful, all of you, he is slippery," Donovan said, Angus started his bike, then Malachi, as he put the shotgun and picture frame into his saddlebags, Duke climbed into the SUV with O'Malley, and they all headed off.

"You be careful, T, the family needs you," Jock said sharply as two black vans and MacBride's sedan pulled up, Donovan accepted Jock's comment with another slap on his shoulder, and Jock laughed. They may not have always gotten along, but Jock had

always been a Father figure to him, like Duke, even before he married Sarah.

MacBride, Stein, and Roberts joined them, "We ready?" Donovan asked.

"You sure we have to hit the Club?" Roberts asked.

"Now that Amanda is her victim, I need to make sure the club is safe. We will go in and secure it, if she is there will take her, if not, even better, it's now my responsibility." Donovan explained.

Scott took a long pipe and placed it up against the deadbolt at the back of the club door, grabbed the handle at the far end, like a grip on a bike shoved it into the lock, breaking the deadbolt, and swung the door open. The club was quiet, Stein and MacBride entered first with guns drawn, followed by six other female deputies, and finally Roberts, Scott, and Donovan. Down the brick hallway, around the corner to each room, two deputies crashed into each room, Scott, and Stein into room eight, the 'Hello Kitty' room, but no one was there, all rooms were empty. MacBride led the group around the corner into the main lobby, but still no one was there, the glass cases taped off from the other day, Scott, Roberts, and Stein charged into the fetish pit, but again found it empty.

"Ok, two back down the hallway, two in front of the Fetish pit, rest with me," Donovan ordered as Scott kicked open the ballroom doors.

The club was dead, no one there, but Donovan thought it was too quiet, he ran to the back rooms, MacBride, Stein, Roberts, and Scott followed, the basement door was open. The remaining rooms are open too, with scorch marks, from the fire, she had torched the

rooms, and somehow, she had done this without anyone knowing, "Scott, downstairs!"

She crashed through the door as Donovan turned to the other door across the inner room from the basement, and headed upstairs, and into Amanda's office.

The room was empty like the rest of the club and trashed. The couch and chair set were cut up with white padding ripped out and Annabelle's picture over the fireplace was torn down and cut to shreds and laid on the floor.

"Nothing downstairs," Scott reported returning with them.

"Secure the building, tape it off, no one allowed in," Donovan said as he slowly picked up his Sister's picture and looked it over as MacBride placed her hand on his shoulder, then his hand with scraps.

The large double oak doors stood over twelve feet tall, with the upper section above three feet, 'Sheriff Eugene L. Coon, Jackson Hole Sheriff,' the plaque sat on the door. Duke, O'Malley, Malachi, Hanson, and two other Deputies quickly walked down the red carpet and up to the doors, with a desk set off to their right. McKnight waited and Malachi with his twelve gauge shotgun raised his right leg and slammed it hard into the door, forcing both doors open. The sheriff sat behind his desk, with his blonde secretary, brown pantsuit, leaning over, he looked up, "What is the meaning of this, O'Malley?" Coon yelled.

O'Malley placed the warrant on his desk, "You are under arrest for cooking the books all those years ago," Duke pushed him down on the desk, and pulled his cuffs out.

"I will have both your shields for this!" Coon yelled and the Secretary ran out.

Duke's handed his cuffs to Malachi, "I think this is all yours, Bro," Duke said.

Coon turned his head slowly and looked at Malachi, "Who the fuck are you?"

Malachi slammed him down and cuffed him, "This does not happen here in Jackson Hole! Remember that is what you kept telling me back then—the closer I got?"

Coon looked back up at him slowly, "Malachi, how, I killed you!"

O'Malley laid a second warrant on the desk, "murder and conspiracy, in the attempted murder of Lieutenant Malachi A. Donovan."

Malachi and Duke walked him out, "I'll kill you! I shot the window out and slammed you into the tree. You're dead!" The Coon yelled. Coon looked up at McKnight, who was leaning against the doorframe with a big grin on his face. "Hey, Boss."

Duke and Hanson walked him out of city hall in front of everyone, and the staff was applauding.

 Malachi shook O'Malley's hand.

Grant stood facing the wall, Donovan opened the cell, and stepped in, "Ok, what are the codes?"

He turned slowly around and faced him, "My deal?"

"Your deal?" Donovan laughed, "If this works, I will talk to the DA."

Grant laughed and paused for a bit, "In the library, above the mantel, find the book, 'Oliver Twist,' Pull it down, it's a leveler. The wall next to the fireplace will slide back with a huge safe door. Enter 7 5 8 8 into the pad, and the door safe will slide open."

Donovan laughed again. "Slut? Hmm . . . and the other safe room,"

"In the old Lady's room, above the fireplace, right candle holder, pull down, 7 5 8 8, again." Donovan nodded and left.

"My deal!" Grant yelled.

The Sherman Estate sat by itself on the sandy soil, there were cars around the fountain, MacBride and Roberts pulled up in the sedan with the vans behind. Stein and a few female deputies ran up the stairs. Many cars around the Estate, it was dusk with lights on in the house and they could hear the commotion of the party.

Donovan could hear the party on both floors. Donovan walked slowly up the stairs, and pulled his SIG, and waved at Stein and Scott at the front doors, they opened it slowly, the foyer was empty, they moved in, and heard the party from the room on their left.

Malachi strolled in behind them, Donovan saw him and nodded, there was no way his father was going to be out of this after all, that had happened thirty years ago. Scott and Stein stood on either side of the rolling doors, Donovan with his SIG, and Malachi with his three-fifty-seven magnum long barrow. Donovan waved to MacBride and four other deputies to move upstairs, She nodded, and they rolled back the doors and ran in with guns held high, other Deputies behind.

Old Lady Sherman sat in her wheelchair nude at the far end of the room by the fireplace, women between eighteen and fifty were sitting, standing, and lying around the room, nude, topless, or half-dressed. Donovan does not see any young girls at present, as Malachi stools slowly up to the old Lady, "Donovan,

what the fuck is the meaning of this," Old Lady Sherman yelled.

"The meaning of this, Ms. Sherman is you under arrest for rape, sexual abuse, and murder of young girls going back thirty-some-odd years," Donovan advised here as he handed her a copy of the warrant. Malachi watched her closely, as Donovan skimmed over the bookshelves above the fireplace.

"Well, I never," she said and turned her chair around to face him fully, as he pulled down the book, and all watched the side bookcase side back into the wall, "How dear you!"

"How dear I, Ms. Sherman," Donovan said as he typed the code, "how dear you!"

The large safe door slid back and revealed a room with six young girls, ranging from seven to twelve, nude, all white, and chained to the walls, with only dog bowls for water and food. Each girl was scared, underweight, and abused.

Malachi stooped down next to Old Lady Sherman and pushed the brim of his hat up with the barrel of his gun, "I had you thirty years ago, old lady, but you stopped me, now it's over. Look at me Bitch!"

Old Lady Sherman turned slowly back toward Malachi, she looked dead into his eyes, and spat, then looked over the old dirty biker, "You, you son of a bitch, the sheriff told me you were dead!"

Malachi leaned closer, "Yes, you fucking whore, he told me that when we arrested him earlier today, and he told me, you paid him, two million to get rid of me and my Granddaughters."

Old Lady Sherman became so frustrated she was speechless. One young girl ran out of the room, across the library, past Scott, and out of the Estate, Scott took off after her, and ran into Hanson, holding the naked girl in a black blanket, he handed her over to Scott.

The whole Jackson Hole County force was now around the outside of the Estate with the North Mammoth motorcycle gang around them, waiting, with Duke and O'Malley at the bottom of the steps.

Scott moved back inside with the young girl, she held her close, and the girl was still crying. MacBride came down with three other girls covered in white sheets, two deputies carrying the other two, MacBride entered the library, and saw Malachi arresting Old Lady Sherman, cuffing her to her chair. MacBride handed the child she was carrying to Roberts, hauled Old Lady Sherman off and backhanded hard, and then stepped near Donovan in the safe room, as the others, with Stein arrested the women and covered them.

Stein pulled a few sheets off the floor and covered the young girls, as Roberts looked on, Donovan returned to Old Lady Sherman, "Where is your Daughter and Granddaughter?"

Old Lady Sherman looked up at Donovan and back at Malachi, "Daughter is upstairs, and Jacki is in the basement, you bastards!"

Donovan looked over at MacBride, she was shaking her head, no, telling him, she was not upstairs, Malachi raised his gun as if to hit the old woman, but Donovan stopped him with his hand up. Donovan stooped down, "I am going to ask you this one more time, Ms. Sherman, and hopefully you will give me the truth, or I will let my father loose on your ass, and just walk away."

Old Lady Sherman looked up at Malachi, and then over at MacBride, who was helping Stein and Roberts, who were carrying the girls out of the safe room as other deputies were walking the women out.

Donovan looked back down at her and then turned to leave. He stood up and took a step.

"Wait!" Old Lady Sherman said, and Donovan turned back slowly, as Malachi raised his gun some more, "Yes, Jacki is in the basement, I do not know where my daughter is, she should have been back by now, with a few new ones."

"Pops, please escort Ms. Sherman out," Donovan said.

Malachi nodded, and looked down at Old Lady Sherman, "My pleasure," Malachi smiled and started pushing the old Lady out of the library, as Donovan and Stein moved to the back of the staircase, at the back of the foyer, behind the stairs, as the remaining deputies walked the women and girls out, behind Malachi.

Donovan opened the door slowly, and ran down the stairs, jumped around the post, with his gun out, "Freeze!" Stein followed and held her gun on Jacquelyn.

Jacquelyn was kneeling over Amanda cutting her, she jumped forward with the knife in hand toward Donovan, yelling, he fired, three shots and hit her dead center in the chest, and she fell back onto the ink machine, hard, and then back onto the floor. Robin started shaking, fiercely, Donovan took off and jumped over the first table, "The device!" Stein yelled.

Donovan pried the devices out of Jacquelyn's cold dead hand and checked her pulse, "She's dead," Donovan checked Robin's pulse, and started pushing down on her chest, Stein moved to help, and Amanda watched them administer CPR, as Roberts and MacBride joined them.

Roberts moved to Amanda, as she coughed through the ball gag, Roberts removed it, Donovan untied Robin as she coughed again and moved to Amanda, untied her, pulled the blanket next to his feet, and covered her up, Stein covered Robin with a blanket, she sat on the floor near her. Amanda grabbed Donovan and held him tight as MacBride removed her gag, "Thank you," Amanda was still crying.

Donovan carried Amanda out the front door, followed by Stein who carried Robin, with Roberts's help, with MacBride followed, Paramedics ran up to the base of the stairs with gurneys, which Stein and Donovan placed the women on them.

Donovan walked over to Old Lady Sherman and heard whistling. He looked up and saw Ferguson and Angus, with the Daughter and a nurse, while Hanson cuffed the Daughter, down the hill near the entrance of the Estate, and both smile. Malachi wheeled Old Lady Sherman away, who was still screaming. Donovan saluted Angus and turned to see Stein she climbed into an ambulance with, Roberts.

MacBride stood next to Donovan, "it's over, right?"

Donovan smiled as the remaining deputies ran in and secured the Estate, Duke walked up, and offered his hand, Malachi returned to them, and slapped Duke on his shoulder, smiling.

All were back at the Roadhouse Marci was helping Jock at the bar, but being more of a pain, but he loves her, the brothers shooting pool in the back, Duke was just coming in, Roberts, Stein, and Scott were drinking, and talking in one of the back booths.

Sarah noticed Gina was sitting on the floor pushing a large red ball across the floor to Frankenstein, who was also on the floor, her Motherly instincts kicked in, and slapped Donovan on the shoulder, who was talking to Hanson next to him.

"You think that is safe," MacBride asked, as Donovan turned and saw where she was pointing, and saw Gina and Frankenstein, playing ball.

Donovan laughed, "No worries; Pops has an eye on her," he said, pointing back over to a table off to the side, Malachi sat with a leg up on the table, Judge Wilkinson next to him in a little black dress. McKnight slapped Malachi on his shoulder, Malachi stood up, raised his glass, and pushed his hat up with his other the hand, toasting Donovan and watching Gina. "Donovan!"

They all turned raised their glasses, toward Donovan, "Donovan!" and toasted him.

Donovan took MacBride in his arms, kissed her, and they danced, as others danced, near them to the music, and others walked by, congratulating him, all having a good time. Jock started clapping, and the others join in, MacBride and Donovan look back toward Jock and smiled. Sarah knew her family was complete again, and she could be happy.

T. K. Donovan Will Return.